SCARRED

(Mikhael & Alina: A Savage Trust Romance)

C.M. WICK
CHRISTA WICK

Published by Evergreen Books Publishing
Copy edits and line edits by GBI Author Services
Proofreading by Rosa Sharon
Cover design by Violet Duke

Previously published as Moskva by Christa Wick (c) 2016.

BOOK DESCRIPTION

Growing up, he was her only protection from the violent crime syndicate their families bore them into, and she his only source of joy.

Her first love, the only person to love her at all.

His reason to exist, the one person he'd risk everything for.

That was ten years ago.

He never knew she'd protected him the only way she could by refusing to escape with him then.

And she never knew he'd survived the fire set to kill him despite her sacrifice.

It isn't until her name appears on a kill order ten years later that Mikhael finally learns of the decade of torture Alina has suffered at the hands of a man more evil than even he realized.

But rescuing her is just the beginning.

Now, with secrets too painful to reveal, and the horrors from her imprisonment still shackling her psyche, the only question left unanswered between them is whether the scars she bears are too deep for even his love to heal.

The SAVAGE TRUST Series
Wrecked (Luke & Marie)
Scarred (Mikhael & Alina)
Frayed (Trent & Daniella)

Previously published as Moskva (c) 2016, revised throughout with newly added content, new characters, and a different extended ending.

MIKHAEL

Russia – Present Day

HIDDEN IN THE SHADOWED DOORWAY OF AN abandoned shop, Mikhael Nazarov watched as his target left a small grocery store carrying a bag of costly oranges. Smiling broadly, her wide hips swinging with her good mood, she walked two stores down and entered a bakery, the door chimes audible from where Nazarov stood on the opposite side of the street.

Nothing about the woman's appearance suggested she had a contract on her life. Her clothes were cheap and simple. She didn't wear makeup. A thick braid down the center of her back restrained her long, dark hair.

He wondered for one fleeting second what she would look like all done up. Clothes that flattered her

1

curves, a little color on her pale cheeks, her hair free and trimmed by a hand other than her own.

Snapping back to the moment, he scanned the sidewalks and entrances, then the windows above the shops. His chest grew tighter with each second that passed. For three days, he had followed her. Every day was the same. She left the walled compound of a former monastery with only a single guard in tow, setting out on foot with a big smile and a bounce in her step. She stopped first at the grocer for fruit, then continued to the baker, where she paid the man extra and waited while he custom decorated two jumbo sized cupcakes.

Her guard, a soft, lazy male whom Mikhael placed somewhere in his late fifties, was just as predictable.

Glancing at the corner, he confirmed the man had stepped into the poorly disguised whorehouse to get his own cupcake frosted for the ten or so minutes the woman would remain in the baker's before she was ready to return to the compound.

Mikhael casually pushed away from the building and started across the street. He wore jeans and steel-toed hiking boots topped by a hooded sweatshirt roomy enough to conceal the Glock 20 nestled against his hip. The hood was down. Small beads of sweat from the late summer heat in Moscow dotted his freshly shaved head.

His gaze stayed locked on the woman, but his ears

were tuned to the sounds of the street. He listened for the occasional car or a sudden change in the low hum of activity as mostly women went about their errands for the morning.

The target's smile never faltered. It was there when she left the compound, its intensity building as the baker started to decorate the cupcakes, the act producing an unexplainable giddiness that made her shoulders shake.

Nazarov knew it wasn't the sweets that excited her. Food had never been the cause of Alina Rodchenka's full waistline. The luscious curves that made his mouth water as he approached the bakery had been there since childhood, her father's attempts to starve them off always failing.

He turned over the fact that she never left with just any two cupcakes. They were specially decorated each morning after her arrival with a different design judging by the changing colors. Her smile would build during their manufacture to an expression of pure joy in a way that hurt Mikhael to his marrow.

It was not the treat that made her glow with happiness, he concluded, but the other person whose teeth and lips and tongue would consume the spongy cake and sweet icing.

Reaching the door to the bakery, he dipped his head and chastised the jealousy that flared inside him. Did he really want to find her after ten years and see her miserable instead of smiling?

She was not his widow, even if they had once been lovers and she thought him dead. She was not his sister, either, even though they had spent part of their childhood growing up together in the same house, Mikhael protecting her within the vicious crime family that claimed them both. In her own way, she had protected him, too, her innocent affection offering comfort in a home where no other kind words or gestures were tendered.

Oblivious to the danger around her, Alina didn't look in his direction when the door chimes announced his arrival. The baker did, his expression deadening as he took in Mikhael's size and the dark shades that hid his eyes. The old man's gaze darted toward Alina in warning, but her attention was on his hands and the wave jumping dolphin he had been drawing.

Mikhael touched her elbow, just the lightest whisper of flesh on flesh. An electric current sizzled through his fingertips and up his arm. There was no similar effect on the woman, at least not that he could see. She adjusted her stance as if the contact had been accidental.

When Mikhael didn't move, she looked up, her smile faltering when she saw the grim slash of his mouth. Her dark chocolate gaze darted around his face, attempting to piece together the features into someone she recognized. When he tilted his chin toward the floor and the sunglasses slid down, she saw the stark blue eyes and her smile crumbled completely.

"Mishka?" she whispered, calling him by his pet name as she had so long ago. No one ever used the Russian nickname for Mikhael before Alina. No one after her, either. Hearing it now uttered in the voice he still heard in his dreams hit him much harder than he thought it would.

He didn't have time to explain. The baker would sound an alarm if the man hadn't already triggered something electronically. Her guard, as lazy as the old slob was, would soon exit the whorehouse and light a cigarette. By the time the fast burning Russian tobacco was done, he would expect Alina to have finished with the baker and be almost to the corner where he waited.

"We're leaving out the back—"

She shook her head and began digging in her purse. "You are leaving!"

Reaching past the rubles in her purse, she pulled out hundred dollar bills, her luminous eyes wide and pleading with the baker. Naively, she was trying to buy his silence in an area of Moscow brutally controlled by the Rodchenko family.

Mikhael knew the man would pocket the money then sell her out within minutes of her leaving. None of that mattered if Mikhael managed to get her out the

5

back door and into the van he had parked at the end of the alley.

"Not without you," he growled, his big hand circling her elbow and locking it in a hard grip. Lowering his mouth to her ear, he whispered as he crowded her toward the swinging door that led into the bakery's kitchen. "Little devil has a kill order on you."

"Little devil" was their childhood name for Dima Rodchenko, the only legitimate child of Papa Rodchenko and the current boss of the Rodchenko crime family after the old man's death eight years ago. Groomed by his father to one day lead the family, Dima was already a full-blown psychopath at nineteen when Papa Rodchenko claimed Mikhael's mother as his in-house mistress.

For a few fleeting seconds, Alina stopped resisting. Fear replaced the vague panic that had filled her eyes upon recognizing her childhood friend and former lover. Then her gaze hardened to black agates and she pushed back, throwing every pound packed into her plentiful curves against him as he had taught her to do so long ago.

"I cannot leave him," she choked, her protest ending with a quiver of lips and tears swimming in her eyes. "Go now before they kill you!"

Her words stabbed at his chest. He had expected a moment's resistance spurred by almost eleven years of thinking him dead. But he didn't expect her to fight back, didn't think he'd see her hand curling around the slim neck of a metal cake stand, the dark eyes warning him that she would pound it into his skull if she had to.

Releasing her, he pulled back. However much things had changed in the last decade, he didn't expect her to cling to a half-brother who wanted her dead, especially since Mikhael was no longer a mere boy but a man battle-tested when it came to taking down scum like the Rodchenko crime boss.

He had to convince her the danger was real and that he could protect her.

"Dima has arranged to have you assassinated—"

The door chimes rattled as the front door of the bakery was slammed open. Alina lifted the cake stand and hurled it past Mikhael's shoulder as she tried to side step around him. He spun, pulling out the Glock as his other hand reached for Alina.

His fingers grabbed at empty air. She stepped in front of Mikhael, her back to the thuggish guard who had finally abandoned his whores and cigarettes to check on his charge.

"Go! Now!" she screamed, her face purpling from the tears she refused to cry. "I won't leave him for a ghost!"

The guard had his gun out, its tip pointed at the middle of Alina's back, her body serving as a shield for each man. Mikhael backed slowly toward the door to the kitchen, his eyes begging, willing the woman to move, to give him a shot at the guard who didn't give a shit if he needed to shoot through her.

Shaking her head, she stretched her arms out, bracing one hand against the counter and the other against a bread rack.

With no other choice that wouldn't result in Alina's immediate injury or death, he hurled his body through the swinging door to the kitchen, slid across a table of cooling pies and burst out the alley's back door at top speed. Lungs burning as he pumped his long legs, Mikhael passed the accuracy range of the guard's pistol by the time the old man reached the alley and fired off his first wild shot.

Diving into the van, he jammed the key into the ignition, turning it as he threw the vehicle into reverse and peeled out of the alley. He headed east, toward Moscow's center where he could dump the van, find another vehicle and start the task of saving Alina from her psychotic half-brother all over again.

Whether or not she wanted him to.

2

MIKHAEL

A MEATY FIST CONNECTED WITH THE SIDE OF Nazarov's jaw. His head snapped left, blood from earlier blows to his mouth spraying the air. The heavy metal chair he was tied to began to tilt from the force of the punch. He threw his weight toward his abuser, the man the others called Osip. He managed to right the chair just in time for a second, more vicious punch. His head and the chair shot a hard left.

He hit the ground, his upper arm pinned between the chair's metal frame and the concrete flooring of the industrial building in which the three men held him.

"Nice one," a thick voice slurred.

Kostya delivered the compliment, his Russian almost incomprehensible to Nazarov because of the heavy accent and the frequent convergence of his mouth with the bottle of vodka he had purchased while fetching the men's dinner.

"Too nice."

This last voice was younger than the others, the few words more precisely spoken and belonging to Arkady, the "brains" of the trio consigned to sit on Nazarov until Dima Rodchenko returned to Moscow from a syndicate meeting in St. Petersburg.

The fact that they had freely used one another's names, both first and patronymic depending on the exchange, only solidified Nazarov's understanding that they considered him a dead man.

Feet appeared in front of his face. Bracing for the inevitable kick, he twisted his neck and upper torso so that his closed eyes pointed toward the floor and not the incoming boot.

Waiting for the impact, he counted off the breaths he took, his nasal passages clogged with blood from a nose broken just that morning.

Nothing happened. They were playing with him, waiting for him to turn his head. They had nothing but time and no entertainment beyond torturing him. They were on their third day of it, ever since eight of the bastards had surrounded his replacement vehicle less than a day after his attempt at kidnapping Alina at the bakery.

"He's going to die before Rodchenko gets here,"

Arkady cautioned. "You know he wants to finish the job himself."

Mikhael cautiously turned his head to look at the young man. With his right eye swollen almost completely shut, he could make out little more than the shape of Arkady's narrow head and upper torso against the ballast light behind the man. Unlike Osip and Kostya, he was slight and hadn't done anything physical against Mikhael. Most of his time had been spent walking around the room trying to get a signal for his smartphone.

Leaning over, Osip tugged the chair upright. "Can't help it if I'm good at my job."

"You better," Arkady warned. "Rodchenko will be primed to kill. What happens if all we have to show is a corpse?"

Osip leaned forward, his hand cupping Mikhael's balls and threatening to rip them off as he put his ear close to the beaten man's lips and listened to him breathe. Blood gurgled in Mikhael's throat. He coughed, splattering Osip's ear with blood.

"Fuck! Fuck! Fuck!" Osip yelled, his big hand closing around the top of Nazarov's skull, the fingers splayed wide, their tips digging at flesh and bone as he hyperextended his victim's neck and wrapped his other hand around Nazarov's throat. "Son of a whore!"

Nazarov squeezed out one word before Osip cut his air off completely.

"Money."

Osip laughed and tightened his grip. "What, so I can have a tsar's funeral?"

Too drunk for caution, Kostya slid away from the wall and nudged Osip's hand away from their prisoner's throat.

"Let us pretend I find this conversation amusing," he said with a vodka lisp.

Retreating, Osip shoved his fists into the pockets of his loose cargo pants.

"I can get you millions," Nazarov wheezed then added. "In dollars."

He wasn't lying, but they couldn't exactly fact check him from the rundown building.

Even if they didn't accept the offer, he reasoned, it might buy time for his body to recover and the punch soup of his brain to come up with a better plan. He had been absent from his job with Stark International, an American security firm, long enough for his powerful boss and friends to start looking for him. He just had to get at least one of these three jokers to spread his name around or try to access the bank account his employer monitored.

Arkady came to stand over him, the young man's green gaze staring into the neon blue of Nazarov's good eye.

"As Osip said, corpses don't need money. You can't give us enough to keep us alive. And unless you have it laying around in paper, which you clearly don't, you can take it back with a few keystrokes."

Half certain he was flinging himself from the frying pan into a volcano, Nazarov offered an alternative— one that would certainly force them to communicate with someone outside the Rodchenko family syndicate.

"Ever hear of Rodya Kalinin?"

Arkady's face lit with speculation. "You mean the fucking rat who almost crippled the Volkovs a couple years back?"

Almost?

Muscles painfully pulled the corners of Nazarov's mouth into a smile. Arkady's assessment was an under-statement. Even the head of the Volkovs, old Vanya with his perpetually bloodstained fingers, had spent time in a Russian prison with all the information Kalinin had turned over to the Russian prosecutors. Their U.S. operations had been wiped out completely.

"What's so fucking funny?" Osip asked, hand leaving his pocket to wrap once more around Nazarov's throat.

"I am Kalinin," he answered, his pain momentarily abated as shock spread across the faces of the three men holding him prisoner. "And whether you pieces of shit want to save me for your boss or sell me off to the Volkovs, you better get me a fucking doctor."

MIKHAEL

New York City – Ten Years Ago

THE BRIGHTLY COLORED CURTAIN ON MIKHAEL'S bedroom glowed pure white as lightning flashed above the city. He counted, waiting for the thunderous boom that must follow. When he reached six, the window rattled.

On the previous lightning flash, he had reached a count of eight. The storm was moving closer and growing in intensity.

Soon she would come, his Alina, her phobia driving her out of her bed and into his as it had done since he was fourteen and she was eleven.

Only she wasn't eleven anymore. She was nineteen, her body deliciously ripe with a woman's curves, her hips and thighs providing a thick and muscular base to support her heavy, full breasts that jutted from her chest. The innocent, small pucker of her mouth had turned equally voluptuous, her pale mauve lips meant to be bruised with a man's kisses.

She was everything he desired and the only woman truly off limits.

Her father, Dmitrey Rodchenko, was a Russian crime boss. He ran half of Moscow and several New York boroughs. Tendrils of his empire spread up and down the Atlantic seaboard. Drugs, prostitutes, gambling, protection money—if a penny could be gained by brute force or illicit pleasures, Rodchenko squeezed with an iron fist.

The old man took whatever he wanted for as long as he wanted. Alina's mother was one of his imported prostitutes. He had kept the woman locked in a room for two years so he could have her whenever he wanted her. When Alina was born, he left her to rot in a whore house until she turned nine.

Mikhael's mother was pulled from the Moscow slums and brought to New York within weeks of her husband's death. Rodchenko tried to leave Mikhael behind, but Kata Nazarova withered without her son.

Now Kata was dead and it was clear the old man wanted to shed all the baggage she had brought with her. Mikhael would have left already but for Alina and the danger surrounding her.

Floorboards squeaked in the hall outside his room.

Mikhael closed his eyes and prayed that she wouldn't knock.

He knew she would. Rodchenko and his psychotic son, Dima, were out of the city for a few days to formally introduce Dima as the heir apparent of the old man's criminal empire. Most of the household staff would be in bed except for a few guards who were supposed to be at posts scattered around the three-story townhouse but were likely clustered at a table playing cards and drinking from the old man's walk-in wine cooler.

A soft knock fell against the wooden door. Mikhael rolled his lips, quelling the temptation to answer. Let her think he was sleeping, he prayed. Let her go back to her room.

The sky lit up again, the whole room glowing. A heartbeat later, thunder so loud he jerked upright cracked the sky.

Alina threw open the door.

"Please, Mishka." Trembling, she stood at the threshold to his room, her long white gown lit on one side from the one lamp at the top of the stairs that remained lit all through the night.

She had fled her room without a robe. The light turned the fabric of her nightclothes semi-transparent, teasing him with the curves beneath the cloth and the dark outline of nipples and pubic hair.

Falling back against the mattress, he brought an

arm up to cover his eyes. He didn't need the temptation of Alina's body against his, didn't need to feel her shaking with fear, the thin linen shift covering her no guard against the heat she generated.

"Go back to bed, little one," he said. "The storm will be out by the harbor in a few minutes."

"It won't," she protested, quietly closing the door and walking over to his side of the bed.

His arm still shielded his eyes. Grabbing his hand with both of hers, she lifted it up, forcing him to look at her as another flash of lightning brightened the room. Her arms trembled as she braced for the oncoming clash of thunder. When it came, she let out a small squeak and dropped his hand.

"Don't be cruel, Mishka," she begged, hugging herself. "I hardly sleep anymore as it is, not since Kata..."

Trailing off, she knelt next to the bed, her head resting lightly on the mattress. "I'm sorry."

Forgetting his reason for wanting Alina out of the room, he reached over and stroked her hair. She was apologizing for mentioning his dead mother so soon after the woman's demise. It was inconceivable to the girl that he missed Kata less than she did.

Far less. Kata Nazarova had become a ghost long before she died. And she stopped being a mother the day she became Rodchenko's mistress. Mikhael's presence was required as a salve to her conscience. But her conscience didn't extend to making sure that her son was free from neglect or abuse.

Forget lifting a finger to stop Rodchenko from taking a strap to Mikhael's back for some imaginary infraction. Kata couldn't be bothered to bat an eye.

Sliding toward the center of his bed, he tugged lightly at Alina's hair. She lifted her head, saw the space he had opened up and climbed onto the mattress. He pulled the blanket up around her, the inside of his wrist unintentionally grazing the point of her nipple.

She stopped breathing at the contact, restarted only after he had the blanket all the way up to her chin.

Let the storm pass quickly, he prayed.

For months they had been dancing around their growing attraction to one another. It would not be long before everyone started to notice. Dima, her demon half-brother, had long accused him of lusting after the girl, even when carnal desire had played no part in Mikhael's love for her.

Now Dima was criticizing everything Alina did, threatening to send her to work with her mother if she didn't stop acting and dressing like a slut—his demented mind warping his perception of the outfits her father clothed her in.

"You're shaking," Alina said, turning on her side and planting one dainty palm against his bare chest. "Have I infected you with my fear?"

"No," he rasped.

Rage made him tremble. Nothing about Alina was slutty. Dima was only blaming her for his twisted desires.

What would the bastard do if he knew Alina had visited Mikhael's room while he and his precious papa were in Atlantic City?

Grabbing hold of Alina's hand, he rolled onto his side to face her.

"You can't stay and you can't come back."

Feeling her flinch, he cursed himself for his harsh tone. But soft words wouldn't work with the girl. She'd find a way to talk him out of the command if he sugar coated it. She could talk him into or out of almost anything, but not this time. Her safety, even her life, depended on it.

"Why?" she asked, her voice cracked and trembling.

"Don't be dull," he answered sharply. "Do you think your papa will save you if Dima wants to send you away? And what do you think Dima will do before that? You know where you will go. Why shouldn't Dima break you in first?"

She tried to free her hand from his grip but Mikhael held on tight in his anger. Relenting, she relaxed into him, her body wracked by silent sobs she was too proud to voice.

Damn it, he should have let her go when she tried to pull free. Now her soft curves were molding around his arm and against his chest. The heat of her body penetrated his. He could smell the mix of berries that scented her shampoo and made his mouth water.

He tugged his hand away and tried to slide to the far side of the mattress.

"We can leave," she whispered, stopping him cold. "The two of us together."

He could leave. He had already taken steps to clear the way. That he was still in Rodchenko's house was only because the man would lose face among the other bosses by tossing Mikhael out so soon after Kata's funeral.

Mikhael lingered because of Alina and a need to earn as much money as he could before he escaped Dmitrey's influence.

"I can't keep you safe," he answered after a long pause. "Not yet."

Keeping her safe would require new identities, ones created by someone outside of the Russian mafia that polluted America's east coast. That took money and connections he didn't have. Hell, he had no connections beyond a name at the FBI, some aggressive crime fighter whose assassination Papa Rodchenko had been toying with a few weeks before.

She answered with a soft exhale of disbelief. "You don't want me any more than my mama or papa."

Another quiet sound escaped her, this one loaded

with hurt and her own quiet anger. "It seems only Dima wants me."

Sitting up, she swung her legs off the side of the bed, ready to leave despite the storm raging on.

"You're leaving without me, aren't you?"

He wanted to lie, to say he was staying and that he'd do whatever was necessary to get the old man to keep him inside the family. But lying would only make her hurt that much more when he left.

Reaching across the mattress, he snagged her hand before she could stand.

"The storm's not over."

"It will be out by the harbor soon." She looked at him over her shoulder, the room too dark for him to see her face. "You said so."

"Stay." He didn't want her to leave, not like this, not thinking Dima was the only one who wanted her.

He was not the monster her half-brother was. He loved her beyond the desire he felt for her. She had been his only true friend all these years of living in New York.

"Stay," he repeated, drawing her close, lips parting to claim her mouth in their first real kiss.

ALINA

ALINA MELTED INTO THE KISS, HEAT ERUPTING IN HER chest and stomach. Her hand slipped free from Mikhael's to drape her arms over his shoulders. He cupped her face, his palms and the tips of his fingers callused from the work her father had him perform at the docks for so little pay.

That same work packed his already big body with muscles. She ran her hands from his broad shoulders to his thick biceps. Her nails dug into the unyielding flesh as a moan slid from her mouth into his.

She couldn't remember how long she had waited for this moment, how many times she had brought herself to a silent, straining climax in her cold and lonely bed knowing he was just a few doors down.

When Mikhael started to pull away, his hands

unclenching from the sides of her face, she clung to him.

"Don't stop," she whispered breathlessly.

All the heat that had warmed her torso sank to the valley of her hips, a throbbing ache building as she sought to wrap her arms around his neck and keep him from pushing away.

He wanted this. She was as certain of his feelings as she was of her own. For more than a year she'd seen flashes of the same intense look on his face that she had recognized as lust in other men. Only, with Mikhael, the hard need was tempered by something delicate and fragile that kept her from fearing his desire.

"Don't you love me?"

"Yes," he groaned and buried his face against her neck. "On my life, I love you."

Knotting her fingers in his yellow-gold hair, she pressed closer to him. Forgotten was the storm with its crashing thunder. Only the lightning was acknowledged as it bathed them in its fleeting brightness.

She kicked at the blankets, hungry to see his bare chest and strong arms the next time the storm illuminated the room. When they were free of the bedding, he pushed Alina onto her back, his hands wrapping around her wrists, her fingers unthreading from his hair as he pushed her arms above her head and covered her body with his.

Mikhael planted a row of kisses against the sensitive flesh of her neck. Squirming, she pushed up against his weight, frustrated that he had her pinned down, the pace of his ardor slowing so quickly she feared he would pull away.

"Don't stop," she begged, hips thrusting upward. "Don't ever stop."

"Love," he said, rasping the word in Russian. "We can't..."

Feeling the hard jut of his cock against her soft underbelly, she knew they could. His body already willed it so.

He stopped moving, his hands still holding her arms captive as he rested with one cheek pressed against her chest. Her needy, throbbing flesh couldn't convince him. She didn't think her tears would either.

"You'll leave and it will be someone else I don't want, someone papa orders me to marry or..."

She wouldn't say the little devil's name, not when her body was in a fevered pitch, the pulsing ache between her legs making her thighs wet.

Could Mikhael smell her need? Did the musk of her sex cling to his nose as it clung to hers?

"I love you," she pleaded. "I need it to be you. You don't have to promise you won't leave later."

Only half of what she said was true. She loved him. But she wanted his promise, prayed that if he took her he would have to stay. Her body began to shake and jerk, the pain of his stopping triggering an emotional breakdown.

His head bounced lightly against her breast from the violence of her movements. His arm brushed innocently against her swollen nipple. She cried out at the contact. Having him against her, hard where she was soft, her flesh sensitive to the barest contact between them, was an exquisite torture she never could have imagined.

"Mishka, please. It hurts so bad."

His hands whipped down the bed at her tearful begging. Finding the hem of her nightgown, he shoved it up over her hips. His hand burrowed between their bodies, calloused fingers slipping between her thighs until he found her slit, hot to the touch and drenched. He squeezed the plump flesh, his mouth returning to her neck to suck and kiss and bite.

The painful need between her legs grew, doubled, then doubled again. Her ass rocked against the hard mattress. She tried to part her thighs, to ease his access to all the raw and weeping flesh hungry for his touch.

Her hands and forearms wrapped around his head, caressing and squeezing at his skull. Her chest pushed upward, her breasts heavy with the request that he suck and kiss at them with the same intensity as he did her neck.

Groaning, Mikhael slipped lower down. As his

head passed her belly button, she shimmied the night-gown up and off.

"Here," she urged, uncertain of his destination and wanting his mouth on her aching nipples and his cock buried inside her.

Elbows pressing at her sides, she pushed her breasts up toward his mouth, offering him his choice of feasting on either one. Lightning from the still raging storm filled the room just as his tongue darted out to wet his top lip.

She moaned seeing the tip. Her legs spread at the sight, her thighs pressing at his hips in a silent coaxing.

"Alina—"

Choking on her name, he surrendered to her offering. His mouth latched around one pouting nipple. Each hand seized a breast, squeezing and pushing them together, his cheeks rough with the day's growth of a young man's beard. His breath blew hot against her skin to singe the nearest nipple with its heat.

Feeling the hard press of his cock as it strained against his underwear, her hands pushed between their bodies. The maneuver pressed her breasts closer together, the added pressure teasing a whimper from her throat.

Mikhael groaned at the sound, his body shaking with hers.

Sensing the intent of her questing hands, he lifted his hips and shucked off his underwear. He surfed forward to lick a slow line up her neck as her fingers wrapped around his hard shaft. She gasped at its dimensions, earning a rumbling growl as he bit lightly at her chin.

His big hands grabbed her hips as she stroked him. His fingers pressed in, dimpling her flesh. A shudder running through him, he abandoned one hip and seized a handful of her hair. Their lips touched and then his tongue thrust inside her mouth.

He withdrew, bit at her lip, tugged it as far as it would stretch.

"Fuck," he growled, ending the kiss and burying his face against her neck.

His hand left her hair, glossed down her arm to find one ripe breast. Squeezing, he roughly held it in place despite her squirming so that his mouth could latch onto her nipple. Then his fingers zipped down to dust her hands off his cock.

He released her nipple with a pop then held her arms down against the mattress as he kissed a line from the valley of her breasts, over the curve of her belly, then down to the silken hair covering her mound.

"Mishka..."

She didn't want him to stop, but fear of the unknown turned her muscles tense. She had heard the maids talk about a man having his mouth against a woman's sex, their words more vulgar.

Eating her...

Would it hurt?

"Wh-what are you doing?" she whispered.

"Tasting you," he rasped. "Making you ready."

How could she be more ready than she already was? Her body wept its juices, the muscles down there contracting rhythmically to push out a steady flow.

"You'll like this," he promised, spreading the lips of her pussy wide and settling his mouth over that same sensitive spine with its absurd little dangling hood that she stroked sometimes when she was alone in her room.

Was that it? Was he going to use his tongue as she used her fingers?

A moan tore from her throat, her entire body tingling from the quiver of need that rolled in waves from between her legs.

Chuckling, Mikhael took his first taste, the tip of his fleshy tongue curling to tickle the underside of the hood, then running a few circles around it before finishing with a hard flourish up the spine.

She jerked and he did it again.

On the third teasing circumnavigation of that sensitive button, he slid a finger inside her. She began to vibrate. Nothing had penetrated her there before. Whining, she pushed against him and was rewarded with a second finger. She squeezed at the digits, whined some more as he licked up and down her sex, stopping to nibble until the vibrations slowed and her hips strained upward in a quest to reach her release.

He strained with her, forcing his fingers into an unyielding V despite the tight muscles that pushed in retaliation. Gently he thrust back and forth, fingers twisting. He teased her swollen clit, shook his face side to side when he had the sensitive flesh trapped between his firm lips.

"Mishka...Mishka..." she murmured. Her hips turned wild. She grabbed his head, held his mouth pressed tight against her flesh as her insides sucked and twisted around his fingers. "Oh, yes. Please..."

He sucked hard at her entreaty, his fingers growing rough in the way they twisted and pushed. She could feel them spread so wide inside her, knew his cock would make her feel even fuller with its fat girth.

Turning his head, Mikhael scored his teeth along her slick pussy before covering her clit again, his fingers racing in and out. Then his thumb replaced his tongue, rubbing over and over the swollen spine as lower down his fingers plunged and circled, thinned and thickened, methodically scraping against her soft, swollen tissues that convulsed around them as he went in, out, deeper and deeper until her hips bucked high and froze, her lush body shaking with its climax.

She collapsed against the mattress, the dance of nerves between her thighs and in the aching tips of her breasts making her wiggle and squirm along the bed.

Mikhael pressed her legs apart, his weight transferring to his knees as he crouched in front of her.

His fingers wrapped around his cock, guiding its fat crown to where her muscles danced the hardest. He pushed forward, her flesh slow to yield. She stopped panting and held her breath for long stretches as her body strained to accept him.

"Slow," he groaned to himself.

His teeth dented his bottom lip as he fought for control. Her muscles fought back, tried to push him out with their tightness even as she whimpered and mewled to have all of him inside her.

Her fingers wrapped around his biceps, the nails digging deep enough to pierce his skin.

The contraction that his mouth and hands had caused still pulsed inside her. He waited, bracing himself for when they contracted outward then pushed when they retreated and the resistance fled with them.

Halfway in, he lost the battle to slowly conquer her flesh. He plunged forward, his weight settling against hers. Alina winced once then ardently squeezed her thighs against his hips.

This is what it felt like to be his woman, to be full of him, stretched to the point she didn't know whether she wanted to cry in pain or scream in pleasure.

Pleasure, definitely pleasure.

Her hips began to rock and bounce against his. With his face buried against her neck, he groaned. His body tilted to one side. He pushed her opposite thigh outward, his hand gripping and squeezing.

He took up a slow but building rhythm of thrust and retreat, thrust and retreat. She chased after him with each in and out, her voluptuous frame rolling in sensuous waves. Their bodies dipped and climbed in unison, pushed on and up so that every sensation multiplied as it bounced hot and slick between them.

Mikhael was the first to lock in place. Alina lifted her hips to meet him, her plump mound grinding furiously at the hard muscles of his stomach, the circle getting tighter and tighter until she froze, the soft, swollen tissues continuing to suck and milk at his cock, coiling and knitting around its thick, jerking length as he spilled inside her.

Together, they collapsed.

A smile curling her lips, Alina reached for Mikhael just as lightning illuminated the room one last time, the storm almost completely past.

Seeing no matching smile on his face, she pulled her hand back.

What had changed so quickly?

"You cannot stay," he said, patting around the pillows to find her nightgown. "You'll fall asleep, we both will."

He handed her the gown. She kept her arms folded against her chest, refusing his unspoken order for her to get dressed and leave.

"Kiss me goodbye, at least," she whispered when he continued to hold the fabric for her to take.

"No. You'll get me to let you stay just a few more minutes, then a few more."

Dropping the gown, he cupped her cheek, his thumb stroking softly across the surface.

"We have to be careful," he cautioned. "We live one day at a time at your father's will."

He glanced at the clock to find the hour well past midnight. "He returns this morning from his trip, the little devil at his side. They can't find you here. Neither can their spies."

Alina snatched at her gown, sat up and jerked it onto her body. Mikhael moved behind her and gently tugged her hair free from where it was trapped beneath the collar. His lips pressed against the back of her neck for one fleeting second before he repeated his warning.

"Each day, we decide by our actions—survive or die."

ALINA

Logs burned in the fireplace of Dmitrey Rodchenko's study. Alina sat in the window seat overlooking the back garden. She had been sitting over an hour after being summoned by one of her father's guards to wait for the old man's return home.

Early August, it was too hot for a fire, even a small one, so she had the window cracked open, just enough to give her relief and let her close it quickly. She didn't listen for footsteps in the hall or the cane Papa Rodchenko used only when he was in his house with no one but his children and trusted staff to see his growing infirmity.

Her eyes and ears were devoted to the gate at the corner of the garden, the one Mikhael used to come and go by Papa's orders since he was old enough to leave the house on his own.

Three days had passed since she had fled Mikhael's room in tears. Contact between them was minimal. He left for the docks early and came home near sunset. She could not catch his eye and only once had he touched her, his hand landing on a doorknob the same time as hers.

His thumb had lightly stroked her wrist, just one passing before he withdrew and murmured an apology. When she had looked at his face, she saw nothing to suggest the stroke had been intentional or even meaningful once done.

Downstairs, her father's cane slapped against the bottom riser. She pulled the window shut, but kept her gaze on the gate until she heard her father's movements just a few feet beyond his study door.

She turned in the seat to face his desk but didn't get up to take one of the chairs close to it. He had summoned her more than an hour ago then left her to wait. Another hour might pass before he acknowledged her presence and she would rather not sit so close to the old man when she didn't have to.

Papa Rodchenko entered the room, his focus on his desk. Grigori, who managed the house, followed behind carrying a shoe box. Placing the item on the desk, he took Papa's cane before exiting the room.

After a glance at her father to ensure he was ignoring her, as always, Alina studied the box. Time had aged the cardboard, especially the corners of the lid. The shoes once housed inside it would be barely larger than her own.

She squinted, trying to make out the faded writing.

Boys, size seven.

She had never seen the box before, but its presence filled her with dread. There was no fancy name brand on the side like the footwear her half-brother Dima got when he was younger. And her father didn't need to save shoeboxes to store things in. He had manila envelopes and banker boxes, big filing cabinets, lock-boxes, bank vaults and more.

Hands folded in her lap, she began to pull at the cuff of her sleeves. Like the fire, her long-sleeved shirt was too hot for the weather. She wore it to hide the pinch marks Dima added to daily.

Her arms had been covered in the small bruises the night she crawled into Mikhael's bed. But the room had been too dark and the bright glow of the room with each lightning flash too fleeting for him to see them. Like Papa and the rest of the household, Mikhael didn't know. There was no point in anyone knowing.

No one cared beyond Mikhael—and maybe not even Mikhael cared. If he did, his response to Dima might get him killed by one of Papa Rodchenko's thugs.

So she wore the long sleeves and tugged at their edges whenever tension began to build inside her chest.

A soft scrape of noise from the back of her father's

throat pulled Alina's gaze from the box to the old man's face. The set of his eyes told her he was annoyed with her already, perhaps for not relentlessly studying him and awaiting his cue that she should approach.

Standing, she crossed the room and took the hard wooden seat in which he made all his visitors sit. He had been scribbling in a ledger the entire time and continued to do so. Waiting, she locked her hands together, fighting both the urge to pick at her sleeves and to touch the box that was now so close.

Outside in the hall, she heard the approach of footsteps, the long, heavy stride telling her it was Grigori, the only person in the house besides Mikhael with such long legs, but without the lightness of the young Russian's step.

Grigori stopped, out of view. She heard the creak of metal. She mashed her lips together, fought the urge to roll or bite at them. What Dima was doing to her arms, she had been doing to the inside of her mouth, especially after the night in Mikhael's bedroom.

She looked at her father, a scream running through her head.

Why had he brought her to live with him? He bought her clothes and fed her when he wasn't trying to starve the weight off her. He kept a roof over her head and the heat on in winter. Yet he had never shown her the slightest affection and was often cruel in his words.

Whenever she wondered why he had finally

brought her into his home, she always came back to the same conclusion. She was there so that Dima didn't step too far out of line.

She had been nine when Papa freed her from the dark, rundown building with its crying, drugged women and all the little children running around in rags. Dima, seventeen at the time, was openly arrogant around his father. Now his arrogance, and the violence that always accompanied it, was more veiled.

Hands still locked together, she sank her nails into the fleshy side of her palm. She was nothing to this man, just a token warning to her half-brother that where there was one bastard, there could be others, some of them suitable to take Dima's place as the family's crown prince—the future Pakhan of their criminal enterprise.

Papa Rodchenko finally stopped scribbling in his ledger. She looked up, meeting his brown eyes. Staring at him, she turned cold despite the fire and her long sleeves in the summer heat.

"I have decided, with Kata dead, you will take over hostess duties."

Her nails dug deeper into her palm. Her entire life, she had never worked beyond keeping her room clean. Staff, protective of their jobs, did everything else. Neither was she allowed to work outside the home and who would have hired her with one of her father's thugs always present? She had been caged up her entire life, first in the hellish house she'd been born into and then in her father's, with only a weekly trip to the library allowed on Saturday.

Even her clothes were bought by someone else and delivered to her.

"Grigori will do most of the work," her father added, his voice sharpening as Alina remained silent. "Just as he did for Kata."

Shifting in his seat, he leaned forward. His gaze critically scanned her outfit.

"You will need new outfits, better fitting and not so drabby. He will take you shopping and select the clothes."

She sucked a slow breath in, her mouth starting to tremble at the thought of the new clothes and the complications that might arise from them.

"Of course," she stuttered after waiting too long to respond. "Grigori knows what will please you and Di—"

The old man's face turned to stone as she started to mention her half-brother. She had erringly equated Dima's authority with her father's. In her world, it was true. Papa could have her killed with the snap of a finger, but the old man ignored her most of the time. Dima was the one who had tormented her from the day she arrived until Mikhael had joined the family and stopped the worst of Dima's bullying despite being five years younger than Dima.

"I'm sure Grigori will find outfits that please you, Papa," she corrected, one hand sliding below the other on her lap to brutally pinch at her soft thigh. The pain distracted her from the bigger hurt in her chest that threatened to choke her lungs.

"One last thing," Papa Rodchenko said, picking up his pen as he nailed her with his dark gaze. "Nazarov is no longer part of this household. He will no longer live here and you will no longer see him."

Never before had she blurted anything at her father, but she couldn't stop the protest from bursting out. "He is Kata's son—"

"But he is not my son. And Kata is dead." Her father's already narrow face pinched with a waspish frown that turned his eyes to small brown dots. "From the moment he entered this house, he has shown nothing but disrespect."

"He only pushed Dima down that one time," she argued, tugging at the cuff of one sleeve.

Would he change his mind if she showed him the bruises? Would he believe his precious boy had placed them there, that Dima always sought to torment her in some fashion, even in front of the staff, and that only Mikhael's presence kept him in check?

"Papa..." she started. Her lips tried to shape the rest of her plea, but the old man stopped her with his hard, uncompromising gaze.

"You disappoint me, Alina."

He didn't care, never had. It was all about Dima. And it wasn't that their father was blind to the little devil's faults, it was that Dima was the elder Dmitrey's mirror in all things. Their actions, their coloring, their unnaturally thin frames no matter how much they consumed, even the beak of a nose that fueled her nightmares of buzzards ripping out her guts.

When she could finally speak again, she nodded at the old man. "I understand, Papa."

"It is not enough to understand. You must know." The stern features never softening, he pointed at the shoe box. "Open it."

Pulling the box onto her lap, she lifted the lid with a hand that shook. As she had started to suspect, the box belonged to Mikhael and he had kept it over the years to store mementos.

Someone had clearly raided her room as well. The contents were a mix of small tokens she had exchanged with him. There was the glitter-covered card she had made at age eleven wishing him a Merry Christmas his first year in the Rodchenko family. In the valentine from when she was fourteen, she had graduated from signing her cards with "your sister Alina" to merely "your Alina" as her affection for Mikhael suddenly yearned in an adult direction she had not recognized at that tender age.

There were cards from him, too, and a small book of proverbs in Russian that he had taught her how to read. Beneath the slips of paper that marked a decade of their lives were other tokens, like a shiny silver button she had taken from a coat he had outgrown three winters ago and the small bull she had fashioned for him out of copper wire as they both watched Kata waste away from an illness the doctors could not identify.

He was her Russian bull, strong and obstinate where she was weak and compliant. Knowing that tough times would follow if his mother didn't recover, Alina had made the wire sculpture to remind him of his fortitude—and her affection.

Now Kata was dead and the tough times were upon them.

Her gaze drifted from the box to the burning log before moving on to her father.

He nodded, the gesture an unspoken order for what she must do without arguing. Taking the box with her, she got on her knees in front of the fireplace and pulled back the screen. She worked on the smallest scraps of paper first and then the cards. Reaching in for the book of proverbs, she palmed the small bull and let it drop just inside the hearth before feeding the book to the fire. Finishing, she placed the box on top of the flaming log and watched it burn, hoping with each snap and crackle that the little bull would survive.

"Grisha," her father said, calling Grigori who had waited in the hall as her father delivered the bad news and forced her to feed the box of treasures into the fire. "Bring it."

Her stomach, already twisted in knots, turned slick with the need to vomit.

Hadn't the old man tormented her enough? What fresh pain waited in the hall with Grigori standing guard over it?

Had they already hurt Mikhael? Was "it" some part of him, like in the crude stories Dima told her on how the family took care of some of its problems by merely making people wish they had been killed?

Metal creaked again and then Grigori entered the room carrying a rabbit with yellow-gold fur a shade darker than Mikhael's hair. For the first time since her father had sat down, she rolled her lips in worry, her face screwing tight with the urge to cry.

Leaning over, Grigori shoved the rabbit at her limp arms, the creature frozen in fear.

"It is not enough to understand," her father repeated. "You must know. If you speak to Nazarov, he will die. If I catch him trying to speak to you, he will die."

She nodded, her head bobbing rapidly as she hoped against hope her father would stop, that he would see not only the terror in her gaze but her absolute obedience and order Grigori to take the animal from her and return the poor, trembling creature to its home.

"Show me that you know, Alina Dmitrievna Rodchenka."

Her lips pressed together, teeth sinking into them as her head and torso shook.

"I know, Papa. I promise I know."

Rodchenko's gaze grew small once more. "Did I bring the wrong girl home from the slave house? Do you belong among those women?"

"No." She shook her head, the first fat tears beginning to stream down her cheeks. "I am Alina Dmitrievna Rodchenka and I belong here."

Her grip on the rabbit tightened reflexively. The animal began to struggle in her arms. Its small claws scratched at her sleeves to mark the skin beneath. Her gaze on her father, she curled one hand around the creature's neck.

Rodchenko's eyes lit at last with approval.

There would be no reprieve. Not for the rabbit nor from what she must do.

Slowly she began to squeeze. The animal's powerful back legs kicked in terror, tearing the fabric of her shirt and drawing blood in thick streams. It screamed—dear God how it screamed. She didn't know a rabbit could make a noise like that.

"Both hands," Grigori counseled. "You'll only make it suffer longer the way you're going about it. Give it a good twist!"

Bile burned her throat and tongue as she angled her

right hand upside down to cup the underside of the rabbit's head as her left had closed around the back of its neck. Squeezing and turning at the same time, her forearm a bloody mess, she heard a moist snap and the rabbit went limp.

Her body sagged in sympathy. She looked up at her father to see quiet amusement flicker across his aging face. He was both satisfied with her compliance and disgusted by her weakness, she thought.

"Take it down to the kitchen for tomorrow's dinner," he ordered, waving Alina away with his pen in hand. "I paid good money for that damned thing."

MIKHAEL

MIKHAEL EXPECTED RODCHENKO TO HAVE HIS MEN IN the library parking lot Saturday morning as the doors opened, with more of his thugs covering the emergency exits. Any other Saturday, the old man would have sent Alina with no better than two guards. If they were old, they would have snoozed in one of the overstuffed chairs in the sun on the first floor. If young, they would have ignored Alina in flavor of flirting with the petite redhead who served as the children's librarian on the weekends.

But this was the Saturday after half a dozen of Rodchenko's thugs had cornered him on the docks at the end of his shift, their fists and boots delivering a warning to leave the city and stay away from Dmitrey Rodchenko's property—all of it.

With just the clothes on his back, a few dollars in

his pocket and the bank where he kept a secret safety deposit box closed for the day, he spent the night in the park cradling his bruised ribs and thinking of Alina as a midnight storm blew through the city.

Friday afternoon, he bought two bus tickets for Chicago, one for him and the other for Alina. Then he entered the library an hour before closing and found a place to hide, his large frame compressed between the underside of a long conference table and the seats of the chairs he had pushed in.

When the security guard came in a few hours later and swept his flashlight, he saw nothing but empty floor and wooden chair legs. All night long Mikhael stayed like that, his battered ribs screaming fresh agony with every breath he took.

Only once the library opened did he crawl out of his hiding place and pull a baseball cap over his yellow hair he had dyed black before buying the bus tickets.

Alina always came in the morning on Saturday, before the day got too busy and her father became as stingy with his men as he was with his money. Mikhael knew where she would go in the library from the books she would always show him upon her return. Classic literature filled with love and war, longing and loss, always drew her. She favored English authors, but Tolstoy and his contemporaries could be found pressing cozily against one of the Bronte sisters on Alina's nightstand.

Hugging the side of a wall, the brim of the cap pulled down to hide his bright blue eyes, he made his way to the Russian section first, his ears alert to any familiar voices.

Using a small mirror, he looked down the aisle and found it empty. Moving two rows over, he waited against an end cap, his body turned sideways so that no one scanning the rows of books would see him.

Long minutes passed, each one promising a more brutal beating than what he had received at the docks if Rodchenko's guards found him.

How ironic and like the old man would it be to keep Alina at home but send his thugs to the library?

Stuck on the thought, he heard sound in the aisle at last. Checking with his mirror, he confirmed that it was Alina and she was alone. Taking a book from the end cap, he placed it on the floor and eased it into her view, knowing that she would pick it up if she saw it.

He counted the seconds, not sure how long he could afford to wait for her to find it. She might have already selected a few books and moved on.

Edging the mirror out again, he stared at her reflection. She hadn't stirred since he last looked, not even a fraction of an inch. Her hands rested against the spines of several books, her fingers splayed, her face caving in on itself as she stared into nothing.

With a light clearing of his throat, he tried to draw

her attention down the row. No sound answered the attempt, not even a rustling of clothes.

Sucking in a deep breath, he stepped into the center of the row and quickly closed the distance between them. Capturing her elbow, he drew her behind the end cap, her soft body compliant as he tugged and steered.

"Alina, it's me," he whispered, lifting the brim of his baseball cap.

She seemed out of it, drugged perhaps. Had Rodchenko given her some kind of medicine so she would be willing bait?

Cupping one of her round cheeks, he lightly tapped the other to rouse her senses.

"We're leaving now. Do you understand?"

Comprehension began to spread across her lovely face only to shut down an instant later as her gaze turned hard and cold.

"I'm not going anywhere with you."

This was not his Alina talking. It didn't even sound like her voice. There was an edge to it as thin and sharp as a razor blade.

"Leave before they find you."

Whatever her reason for ordering him away, he ignored it. She was afraid, that was all, afraid her father's men would hurt him.

"How many guards?"

"More than a boy like you can handle," she answered, the cadence of her words a perfect match for the Rodchenko men he had spent his teen years despising.

She brushed his hands away and pushed at his chest. Stunned, he let her open up a distance of a few inches between them. Her gaze swept over him, her lips curling with distaste as she took in his clothes wrinkled from a night spent in hiding.

"I have bus tickets for us. There's a window in the break room big enough to crawl through."

Her gaze was as dead as the fish he spent summers carting around in barrels at the docks.

"You don't have to be afraid of your father or Dima," Mikhael coaxed, certain that it was fear fueling her resistance. "We are right by the station—the bus leaves in thirty minutes. They won't be done looking for you in the stacks by the time..."

She tilted her head, the motion robotic.

"How many times did you ask your mother to leave?" she softly whispered, her voice dripping with a false sweetness. "I heard you once, that first month, crying and begging like a little bitch."

Mikhael braced as if she'd hit his already battered body with all her force. His Alina never swore.

"If she couldn't love you enough, why should I?"

He grabbed her shoulders, his fingertips digging at her soft flesh.

"Did they threaten you? Did they tell you they would kill me? Is that why you're saying this?"

It had to be. His sweet Alina would never talk like this. He didn't care how much she looked and sounded like a true Rodchenko at that moment. She was incapable of such venom.

Then how come it flowed so easily off the tip of her tongue?

Her plump lips twisted into a sneer. "I don't care enough to lie to you, Mikhael. If you try to take me, they will kill you. But I don't care if you live or die."

She brought her hands up between their bodies, her palms open and poised for a sharp clap that would draw Rodchenko's thugs. "Shall I show you how much I don't care?"

Releasing her shoulders, he stepped back and shook his head, reality spearing its way through his chest.

Alina was lost to him—if he'd ever really had her at all.

MIKHAEL

Mikhael lingered in the city, the few thousand dollars he had stashed in the security deposit box at the bank dwindling fast. For twenty bucks a night, he got a room in a flop house that was little more than a former closet walled off. No private bathroom, no window, one door, and a sliver of floor between the bed and the wall, was all his money afforded him. Located at one end of the first floor, his neighbor was a hooker whose thrashing and moaning plagued his attempts to sleep. Across from his room was the communal toilet that tenants visited throughout the night.

He stayed in New York because of Alina even though he knew he should have gone straight from the library to the bus station. Escaping the library, Mikhael had spotted four cars in the parking lot that he knew by sight and six perimeter guards working in pairs at all the exits. Rodchenko was serious about his warning to stay away. The old man wanted a reason he could wave in front of the other families for why he "rightfully" killed Mikhael.

Listening to his neighbor and her customer finish their business, he closed his eyes and tried to catch some sleep before she returned with another man to fuck.

His brain didn't want to settle. Should he make a second attempt at the library? If she showed up, did that mean she wanted to see him again? Should he try to get into the house—or at least the yard?

There were two windows that looked out on the garden with its alleyway gate. One was Rodchenko's office window. The other was an alcove in the hall where she liked to read and could almost always be found when he was returning from his day at the dock.

Foolishly, he had fancied she chose the spot to see his arrival home and to have him pass her in the hall on his way into his room. Now he wasn't so sure.

Her barb about his mother had sunk deep.

Within days of his father's violent, unsolved death as an underling in Rodchenko's crime syndicate, the old man had swooped in to make sure the widow Nazarova's needs were being met. Even at thirteen, Mikhael new Dmitrey's visit was unusual. There were other widows and mothers on the street whose husbands and sons had died doing his dirty work. Most were abandoned.

But none looked like Kata with her pale freckled skin, yellow gold hair and sky blue eyes.

She had a beauty that didn't belong in the slums of Moscow. Rodchenko pounced at the first opportunity and carried her away to America. Mikhael had spent the rest of his childhood as unwanted baggage living under the withering gaze and iron thumb of a crime lord and his petty tyrant of a son.

The only thing that had kept him from running away that first year and all the years that followed was Alina. Even though he now knew those years had been wasted, he still couldn't leave, still clung to the edge of the city in a roach infested flophouse with walls so thin he could put a fist through them with a simple morning stretch of his massive arms.

Mikhael maneuvered from laying on his left side facing the wall to his right side, his body too big to sleep on his back in the narrow bed. Finishing his turn, he reached to pull the thin sheet over his shoulders and caught his first whiff of danger.

Smoke—in a five-story tinder box with no working fire alarms and no sprinklers.

He sat up immediately, his bare feet sliding into his work boots as he inhaled deeply. He smelled fuel. This was not somebody's hot plate left on too long, the contents turning to a hardened ash in the pan.

This was intentional.

Having gone to bed in jeans and a t-shirt, he raced to lace up his boots and then he slid on his jacket. He made a quick check of the pockets to ensure his wallet and an old Russian passport were in place. He shouldered the cheap backpack he had purchased at a re-sale shop to hold a few pieces of clothing. The contents didn't amount to much, but it would hurt to lose anything now that everything else had been taken from him.

Other tenants were beginning to flee their apartments, the hall a mix of languages with voices ranging from the very old to the newly born.

Smoke started to pour under and around the edges of his door, the room's air growing painfully thick.

In partitioning the tenement into more units, the slum lord who owned the place had salvaged materials from other buildings. Mikhael's door was metal, one of the sturdiest and the biggest reason why he had picked the room despite it being in a high traffic area because of the shared toilet and stairwell.

He placed his palm against the door's surface. He could feel the heat, hear the crackle of flames. The accelerant fueled fumes turned his stomach sick. He hiked the collar of his shirt up over his nose and used the edge of his jacket as a mitt to turn the door knob.

Fire waited for him on the other side, but there was

no window to crawl out of. Bracing for a blast of heat, he pulled on the door.

It wouldn't budge. The knob turned freely but the door wouldn't open inward. He jerked again, abandoning the jacket to grip the knob with his hand and twist as hard as he could.

Panic building in his chest, Mikhael threw himself at the door. He heard the bounce of heavy metal chains and knew for certain that the fire was set for him. Rodchenko's thugs had warned him to leave the city and he had stayed. The old man was willing to burn down a five-story tenement filled with hundreds of people to carry out his threat against one man.

Backing up as far as the tight quarters would allow, he aimed a kick at the door knob, his eyes beginning to burn and water from the smoke.

The kick was fruitless, not even a groan of protest.

Outside his room, people were starting to panic as tenants from the higher floors streamed into the smoke-filled hall. He imagined all eyes focused on the nearest exit —which was half a building away from his chained door.

There were no heroes in this building. The fire teams would be too slow to reach him. And his time to break through the door was over—he could feel the heat of the fire on his threshold.

A grim laugh burnt its way up his throat. He had bitched and moaned inside his head about the paper thin walls between the units. He hoped like hell he was right about their consistency.

Flipping the bed and frame onto its side, he gained a little distance away from the wall then charged at it, his shoulder leading the way with his forearm up to guard his head. Plaster crumbled. A pipe no more round than his thumb broke at its joint, dousing him with water.

Stumbling against the prostitute's bed, he reached to his right hoping for a window but finding only the exterior wall. Looking to his left, he knew the door out was a last option, the wood already splintering from the heat. Shoving the whore's bed against the wall he had just demolished, he flipped it, threw his arm up again and charged at the next wall between units.

Pain sliced through his hip as another decaying pipe broke, the metal shearing and cutting through his jeans. Ignoring the wound, he turned to the room's single window, tearing down the curtain to find bars welded in place.

He coughed, choking on mucus as the acrid smoke scraped at his throat and lungs. Reaching the door, he touched its surface then seized the knob and yanked. Smoke billowed thick into the room. In the hall, a screaming woman ran past as she exited the stairwell.

Poking his head out, Mikhael looked toward the exit. Blood froze in his veins. Kiril Lapin, one of Rodchenko's *Boyevik* warriors stood surrounded in a soft haze of smoke, a wet handkerchief to his face. With a gun in his hand, he waved the tenants out of the building.

With no more than a few seconds to decide before Lapin turned around and spotted him, Mikhael hurled himself at the stairwell and began to push frantically against the wave of bodies that streamed downward.

By the time he reached the third floor landing, there was no one to push against. He took the fourth and fifth-floor stairs two steps at a time, reaching the roof out of breath and coughing up chunks of soot-filled snot.

Wheezing, he made his way to the edge of the roof and looked down to the narrow alley below. The flames on his corner of the building were about to overtake the fourth floor, the lower floors already beginning to crumble. With the support under his feet in danger of giving way, he dashed to the opposite end and stared down again.

Taking a deep breath, he eyeballed the distance between his rooftop and that of the building across the alley. Eight feet maybe, plus the three foot tall lip on each roof.

Looking down into the alley, he saw more of the building in flames. It wouldn't be long before the fire leapt across the alley and everything under his feet collapsed into rubble.

With no time to practice the distance, he went to the

other side of the roof and started running. Two feet from the building's lip, he sprung upward, his long legs quickly tucking close to his ass as he went airborne over the alley.

He cleared the gap. His knee slammed against the lip on the other building. His right shoulder hit the rooftop, then his face. He wanted to rest, to wait there until his face and shoulder and knee stopped screaming bloody murder.

If he did, he was dead.

Standing, he limped over to the other side of the building and stared at the alley below. No one appeared, not even faces in the window. He scurried down the fire escape, moving from building to building until he was far enough down the street he could step onto the sidewalk without Rodchenko's men spotting him.

A month later, he touched down in Moscow as Rodya Kalinin—the newest recruit in a joint task force between the FBI and its Russian counterpart to stop organized crime.

MIKHAEL

Russia – Present Day

REACHING INTO HIS MEDICAL BAG, THE PHYSICIAN nodded at Mikhael's bloodstained shirt. A faint tremor ran through his hands as he snapped on a pair of blue surgical gloves.

"That will need to come off."

Osip dropped the sandwich Arkady had picked up while fetching the doctor onto a deli wrapper and stood. His hand dove into his pocket to retrieve a buck knife as he strolled over to where Mikhael remained tied to the chair. With a grin smearing his face, Osip opened the blade and grabbed the cuff of Mikhael's sleeve.

Careless with the knife, he began ripping upward, nicking the skin along his bicep and again at his collar.

Mikhael watched through swollen eyes as the doctor turned pale over the rough treatment.

The man was young for his profession, probably mid-thirties. Mikhael doubted he had ever been summoned to attend a prisoner just so that the patient could be murdered later by the same thugs. Any work he did for the Rodchenko syndicate in Moscow was likely at the end of the crime—patching up bullet wounds after gunfights or otherwise saving the lives of killers so they could kill again.

Osip circled behind Mikhael to start cutting on the other half of the shirt.

"Can't you untie him?" the doctor asked.

Leaning forward, Osip stuck his craggy face in front of the doctor's, smiled a leering grin and pointed with his bloody blade at the two teeth Mikhael had knocked out when they had captured him.

It had taken eight of them total to subdue Mikhael. Osip, Kostya and Arkady were left to guard him while the others were treated for broken ribs, a shattered eye socket and a skull fracture.

"I don't think so," Osip lisped.

The doctor bobbed his head, sweat beginning to bead along his upper lip.

"I'll need—"

"Hoy!" Arkady interrupted from where he stood by one of the few boarded up windows that offered cell reception. "Does he have a tattoo on his chest?"

Returning to his sandwich, Osip kicked Kostya where he snoozed on a floor mat.

"They want to know if he has a tattoo on his chest."

Kostya wiped at eyes still bleary from the vodka he had consumed the night before. He rolled onto his feet and shuffled to where several jugs of water were lined up. He grabbed one, twisted off the cap and began to splash it on Mikhael's chest.

Looking around, he snatched up the shredded shirt and used it as a wash cloth, dousing the dried blood with more water as he scrubbed.

"He's got a whole fucking painting!" Kostya bellowed. Leaning close enough that Mikhael could have head butted him, the old Russian squinted at the gray and black shaded drawing. "An angel with a spear stepping all over..."

Hesitating, Kostya poured more water on the tattoo.

"Stepping all over...uh..."

"The devil," Mikhael offered, Rodchenko's name whispering at the back of his mind.

"The devil," Kostya repeated.

"It's him, it's fucking him," Arkady shouted. "He was telling the truth!"

Osip continued eating his sandwich as if nothing had been said. Kostya sank onto his ass and broke into laughter.

"I'll be damned."

Mikhael knew the deal was set. His captors

intended to sell him to the Volkov family for money and a protected place within their organization. With Dima's reputation as an unparalleled psychopath, no one on the side of the Volkovs would question the men's motivation for selling out their boss.

"I may be able to reset this," the doctor said, his fingertips wrapping around Mikhael's strong cheekbones while his thumbs pressed softly at the sides of his broken nose.

"Don't," Mikhael growled. After he had finally spit and snorted out or swallowed down most of the blood-filled mucus, he found he could breathe without difficulty. Resetting his nose would only bring more blood and fresh pain to cloud his mind while he worked on escaping.

The doctor dropped his hands to trace the lines of Mikhael's ribcage. Another growl and the swollen and bruised flesh confirmed a potentially cracked rib.

Grabbing a roll of elastic bandaging, the doctor began to weave a compression wrap around Mikhael's chest and back where the rib was injured. Each time he wound the roll to the front, he had to dip close to Mikhael's ear.

"I have a pill," he whispered, rolled some more and whispered again. "It will wipe out your pain—forever."

"No," Mikhael answered, his voice just as low.

Finished with the wrap, the doctor turned at last to the swollen right eye.

"Can you follow my finger."

Wincing, Mikhael forced his eye to track toward his broken nose then back to center.

"Well, I don't think the retina is detached, yet," the doctor said. "But if the swelling doesn't go down, you could lose your sight in that eye."

Osip grunted a laugh, its meaning clear to everyone in the room—even the physician.

"Look," Arkady said, his call finished. "Fix him up so he's good for a few days. He's someone else's problem after that."

Pocketing his phone, he began to rummage through the doctor's bag. He scooped out five pill bottles and tossed them to Kostya.

"Those are for the sick," the doctor protested, the color draining from his face once again.

"I'm all kinds of sick," Arkady smiled. "I could make a house call and show you what I'm talking about."

Looking at the floor, the doctor removed his gloves and kept his lips tightly pressed.

Finished with his treasure hunt, Arkady snapped the bag shut and shoved it at the physician. "The Rodchenko family thanks you for your service, comrade."

Mikhael watched Arkady shove the doctor's wind-breaker and bicycle helmet at him then lead him to the heavy iron door that opened onto the building's back alley. Mikhael doubted the doctor would be of any additional assistance. The man had to know what would happen to him and his family. Even if he went to the police, he couldn't begin to guess which of the officers wasn't on the Rodchenko payroll.

Getting a doctor had never been more than a bid for time and maybe some electronic chatter. He wasn't a man without friends, friends far more powerful than he was. They had more than enough resources to take on Rodchenko. First, they had to find him—and he hadn't made that easy.

Learning of the threat to Alina, he had been downright stupid about things.

Now he had to be smart. He had to buy as much time as he could, look for his own escape opportunities and push Arkady into contacting Volkov or Dima, even the doctor, as many times as he could. The more chatter, the greater the chance he'd be found or finally haul his own ass out of the shit he had fallen into.

Arkady plopped down on the mat next to Kostya and retrieved one of the pill bottles.

"Just what the doctor ordered," he grinned, popping the lid and shaking two tablets into his hand.

A timid knock sounded at the alley door. Osip cursed then swiped at a drop of mayonnaise on his chin as he stood up and kicked Kostya, who had already taken some of the pills and chased them with more vodka.

"Useless," he grumbled, pulling his pistol from the back of his jeans and stalking toward the door. Standing on tiptoe, he looked through a hole in the boarded up window. "I think he wants his pills back."

"Tell him he can suck my balls," Kostya called, the fingers of one hand dancing in the air as if trying to catch a hallucination.

"Have you seen his wife?" Arkady asked as Osip slid open the last lock on the door. "Now that's a bitch I'd pay to fuck. Hey, Osip, tell him to bring that hot bitch here and I'll give him some of his—"

Thwip-thwip

Mikhael threw his weight to one side, forcing his chair to the ground as the whisper soft firing of two bullets through a silencer dropped Osip to the ground and shut Arkady's mouth. The kid's hands fumbled around his body like he was searching for a gun. All he came up with was his smartphone.

Kostya started to laugh, his finger lazily pointing at Osip's dead body. "Now you're the one sleeping on the job, asshole!"

Thwip-thwip

Arkady's brains exploded out the back of his head, the splatter of blood and flesh finally sobering Kostya. He scooped up the pill bottles and offered them to the man in the windbreaker and bicycle helmet.

"Here!" Kostya begged. "I didn't tell him to take them."

Thwip-thwip

With the last of Rodchenko's thugs dead, the man turned to Mikhael. Sunglasses covered his eyes. Below them, a satisfied grin pushed his bold cheeks up high. Bending down, he whipped the glasses off.

"I guess this makes us even now, Nazarov."

"Not so much, Hades," the Russian chuckled. "But you're finally getting close."

9

MIKHAEL

"Why, when a man goes crazy, it is always about a woman?" Trent Kane, code name Hades and Chief Operating Officer of Stark International, asked from the back of an operations van that looked like it had last been used by a plumbing contractor without being cleaned out.

Mikhael shrugged and reached into the bag Kane had tossed him a second earlier.

"Hold up, don't put anything on yet," Reed Henley, another Stark employee, ordered from the front seat, a computer balanced carefully on his lap and Arkady's smartphone in one hand.

Kane rolled his eyes then leaned against the side of the van and closed them. Mikhael slid along the bench seat and looked over Henley's shoulder.

"I thought you don't do field ops anymore," he said, his injuries turning each word into a rough mumble.

"And I thought you would have enough sense not to run off on your own."

"C'mon," Mikhael joked. "You're old enough to be my granddad. You should be in a home playing bingo with silver-haired ladies."

Snorting, Kane opened his eyes. "Lucky for you that he isn't. Reed's the one who found your dumb ass after figuring out it was this Alina chick who put you on a suicide mission."

Mikhael shot Kane a hard look.

The man was right, though. Mikhael had foolishly expected a different reception. There was no reason to think she wanted to see him, not after everything she had said the last time he saw her. Still, trying to save her life while explaining that Dima had a kill order out on her should have softened her up toward Mikhael a little.

The hurt over how he had parted from her was definitely the reason for his telling no one he was going. He didn't want to relive the past or justify the danger he was putting himself in for a woman who had so coldly rejected him.

"Fine," Mikhael mumbled and reached into the duffel again.

"Hold on, now," Reed said. "You still want to help her, right?"

Mikhael let the shirt fall into the bag. "Yeah. But she doesn't want help. She said she won't leave Dima."

"Dmitrey Dmitreyovich Rodchenko?" Reed asked, pulling up a document on his computer. "Current head of the Rodchenko crime family and her half-brother."

Her half-brother and Satan's most evil spawn.

"That's the bastard," Mikhael agreed.

Would it change Alina's mind if he played the recording to her—the one with Dima talking to an underling in a Geneva hotel about getting her to Russia during the Pakhan meeting in St. Petersburg and making it look like a rival within the Rodchenko syndicate assassinated her?

"Well," Reed continued. "If you want to help her, we have a short window of time before anyone knows you've escaped or that you likely had help doing it. Right now, the guards at the compound have returned to business as usual, especially since Rodchenko is not set to return from St. Petersburg until tomorrow. But it could only be hours or even minutes before Dima tries to dial up one of the dead men."

"He knows the reception in that building is shit," Mikhael offered.

Jiggling Arkady's phone at them, Reed smiled. "Good. I have a plan that will have one of Rodchenko's men deliver Alina exactly where we want and then leave her with us."

"And why would he do that?" Kane asked, his gaze lighting up with curiosity.

Reed jiggled the phone again. "Because his boss told him to."

MIKHAEL

MUSCLES ACHING, HANDS LOOSELY TIED BEHIND HIS back, Nazarov sat on another steel framed chair. The building was different, this one a long, narrow unit with an electric roll-up door at the front, no windows, and a smaller exit at the back left slightly open.

Two cameras on tripods pointed at his body, both of them forward from where he sat at the back of the unit, one on the left, the other on the right. Harsh studio lights bathed his body in unrelenting brightness that showed every cut and bruise on his face and bare torso.

The bulbs were hot, making him sweat. He let his head droop. Fatigue weighed him down but the constant stream of adrenaline his body manufactured kept him from sleeping.

Mostly, he didn't want his expected guests to see the hope blazing in his one good eye.

The rolling door at the far end began to raise. He didn't lift his head, knew he had to look defeated.

Through an earpiece, Kane let him know everything that was going on. Reed had sent a text mimicking Dima's phone to one of the guards at the compound, all of their cells pinged to pull their numbers days ago while he and Kane searched the city for any sign of Nazarov. After capturing Arkady's phone, he had matched up the numbers already gathered with names in the dead man's contact list.

With their cell numbers, Reed had been able to hack into some of their phones, read their messages and determine who was the most obedient and gullible. He sent the text to Fedor Gusev with an address and the words "Come alone, bring Alina with you."

Now, with the door open, he texted Fedor to let Alina out. The woman didn't fight. She got out of the car clutching her purse before Fedor had time to finish reading the message. She was halfway down the length of the unit before the final text flashed across Fedor's screen as the rolling door began to close under Reed's remote direction.

Go. Leave her.

Hearing the rolling metal door shutting her in, Alina froze. Glancing over her shoulder, she saw the lights of the car disappear. Turning back to face the lifeless looking man in the chair, her shoulders sagged.

Reed stepped through the unit's rear door, his hair

slicked back, sunglasses covering his eyes and black gloves on his hands. He held a pistol in one, the same weapon with its silencer that Kane had used to kill Osip, Kostya and Arkady.

Slowly, he lifted the gun toward Nazarov's head.

"No!" she cried and crossed into the bright lights. Ignoring Reed disguised as a gunman, she wrapped her hands around one of the cameras and started to beg. "You don't have to do this. I am loyal to you."

Tears streamed down her face. Her nose began to run and she wiped absently at it.

"You know you will always have my loyalty. Don't do this to him."

Reaching down, Reed tugged at the knots, freeing Nazarov's hands. The big Russian made it onto his feet, his gait unsteady in approaching Alina as she continued to plead into the camera, promising Dima anything.

When he wrapped his hands around her shoulders, she screamed and fought like a caged animal until she saw that it was him. Then she stopped as sure as if they'd shot her with a tranquilizer dart.

"This is fake?" she said after her gaze skittered around his face then over to Reed to find the gun re-holstered and Kane and another team member entering the room to quickly clear the camera and lights.

"A ruse to kidnap me?" She screamed the accusation, her hand closing into a fist that connected a second later with the cheek below Mikhael's swollen eye.

"Dima is going to kill you and blame Malinovsky," he rasped, doing nothing to shield himself against her next attack.

Her fingers wrapped around the sides of his face, the nails digging in and her thumbs poised to gouge his eyes. Halting, she turned pale. She jerked her hands close to her body, leaned to the side and threw up.

"Time to go," Reed urged as the last of the equipment was cleared from the room.

"Your wounds are real," she said, swiping the back of her shaking hand against her lips.

Scrambling away from him, she pushed onto her feet. "Go home, Mikhael, wherever that has been all these years. You'll get us both killed."

Growling, he advanced on her, his footsteps too unsteady to catch up as she drew further away.

"He already intends to kill you, Alina!"

"Why add another body, you fool?" she asked with a bitter laugh.

"You. Don't. Have. To. Die!" he ground out.

A feeble smile brightened her face. "Maybe Dima will give me one last day with him."

All but broken, Nazarov turned to Reed. The big Russian's hands curled into fists and his arms shook with the need to punch something. "Help me understand, my friend."

"Stockholm syndrome?" Reed offered. "Given the dossier I worked up, she's been victimized her entire life. She's formed a traumatic bond with this Dima character where any brief respite in his cruelty is perceived as—"

"Not Dima," she said. "Never Dima."

"We need to go," Kane warned, popping his head through the unit's rear exit. "Get your asses—and hers —in the van. Now!"

"I'm not going anywhere." Taking another step back, she crossed her arms against her breasts and tucked her chin, her dark eyes threatening a fight. "Fedor will return, eventually."

Hearing Nazarov's sharp intake of air, Reed stepped between them and fished a small vial with a spray cap from his pocket.

"Look, Miss Rodchenko, we can do this the easy way or the hard way." He took a meaningful glance at the unit's concrete floor then smiled at her. "I suggest the easy way."

Her expression widened, the eyes appearing startlingly large with the irises colored a dark chocolate.

Reed lifted the vial higher, its nozzle pointed at her face. He smiled. "Doesn't matter if you hold your breath. It will begin penetrating your skin immediately."

Exhaling, she stepped past him, her gaze scanning the ground for her abandoned purse.

"It's already in the van, Miss Rodchenko," Reed said, his hand against Nazarov's back to get the giant moving.

As soon as they stepped outside and Alina disappeared into the vehicle, Nazarov came alive. Twisting, he slammed Reed against the building's brick wall.

"What was that?" he growled. "I don't want a scratch on her!"

"This?" Reed laughed, taking the vial out and delivering a squirt onto his own tongue. "It's a breath freshener."

Reed pressed the vial into Nazarov's hands. "Not to be rude, buddy, but you might want to take a few shots yourself. You haven't exactly been practicing the best hygiene the last few days."

MIKHAEL

Nazarov entered the van to find Alina arguing with Kane as the man attempted to search her purse.

"This is mine," she said, tugging at the strap as he finished unzipping the bag. "I told you there are no trackers in it."

Nazarov's meaty hand swooped down and claimed the purse from both of them. He shoved one fist in and seized a small stack of folded papers. Fanning a few open, he saw drawings done in a child's style. A dinosaur, a volcano, a dolphin jumping waves.

"No, no, no," she said as he let the pictures fall to the floor. Gathering the pages up, she clutched them to her chest. "Stop touching my things."

He grunted, scooped out her phone and watched her face as he passed the device off to Reed. Still holding onto the papers with one hand, she reached after the phone with the other, her face beseeching Reed to give it back.

"Please, they are all I have..."

"I'll be very gentle with the contents," he assured her, his voice dropping low in an attempt to calm the distraught woman.

Pulling out a box of crayons from the bottom of her bag, Nazarov dumped them on the floor and watched them scatter, then he checked the box for anything taped inside.

Feeling that the purse was empty, he looked inside, saw nothing. Turning it upside down and shaking, he heard a small metallic click as something fell out. Leaning forward, he saw the item. At first glance, it looked like junk. Mangled metal oxidized except for a small inward dipping curve on one side where it must have been rubbed frequently to keep the copper showing through.

He could just make out where the bull's horns attached to the head. He looked at Alina to find her hugging her papers, her eyes on her lap and her face screwed tight from the tears she was holding in.

She had been crying earlier, begging and sobbing at the camera to spare him. And she still carried the little figure she had shaped for him so many years ago. But she wouldn't leave Dima, even if staying meant she would soon be dead.

Pocketing the figurine, he pulled out a knife and

ripped through the fabric of the bag. His fingers manipulated the lining.

"He took all of your money, your identification?"

She said nothing, just continued staring at the top of her knees.

Nazarov passed the bag to Reed, who rolled down his window and tossed it onto the street.

"No point risking it," he explained before he returned to sifting through Alina's phone.

Reed's fingers slowed as he looked through her photos. He expanded one, Nazarov's viewing angle too narrow to see what the picture contained or why it should hold Reed's interest for so long.

"This boy," he said, pointing the phone's display at Alina. "His name is Bogdan, yes?"

She nodded, her hand reaching for the phone, her fingers engaged in an urgent dance to coax Reed into surrendering the device.

Nazarov snatched it up, expanded the photo and stared at the boy. His head was tilted downward, black hair covering his eyes. The shade was that of all the Rodchenkos he had ever known. Alina, her father, Dima.

White and blue frosting smudged the boy's sharp chin.

"Dmitrey Rodchenko's son," Reed offered, his laptop out and opened once more. "No photos publicly in existence, his location more secret than his father's although presumed to live in the States. Mother unknown, rumored to be from one of the slave houses."

Reed dipped his head so he could look into Alina's flat gaze. "Is Bogdan why you're fighting us?"

Her shoulders scrunched together. Pursed lips trembled and her hands shook as she tried not to crush the drawings in her hand. She looked at Reed, the muscles of her throat visibly tightening.

"Please, it's like the hospital, isn't it? If I don't want help, you cannot force it on me."

Reed retrieved the phone from Nazarov. He swiped through more of the photos. Stopping at the last one, he looked from the photo to Alina before studying Nazarov for a few long seconds. His brow lifted, skeptical, and then he shoved the phone in his jacket pocket.

"What if we kidnap the boy?" Reed asked.

"Hold up," Kane interjected. "We have no reason to believe the boy is in danger. There are scummy parents all over the world. Law doesn't let us kidnap them."

"What fuck should I give over Dima's bastard?" Nazarov grunted, his gaze hard on Alina.

If only she had left with him that day at the library. They'd have children of their own. She wouldn't be risking her life over Dima's brat, a boy that would one day grow up to be as cruel as his father.

"Rodchenko plans on killing a family member to cement his position," Reed argued with his gaze on

Kane. "If it isn't his bastard sister—no offense—then all that remains to sacrifice is his bastard son."

Nazarov nodded. Dima had a sickness in him. The pain of others was his entertainment.

"Please," Alina whispered. "You see now why you have to let me go. Bogdan cannot take my place in Dima's plan."

"He will fucking kill you!" Nazarov screamed, his hand shooting out. He tore the papers from her grip and began tearing them up with each new word that came out of his mouth. "First he'll have them beat you. Rape you. Stab you. They will cut off toes and fingers, make your tongue a stump."

When the child's drawings were reduced to confetti, he looked at Reed for confirmation. "You listened to the tape, the one recorded in King's hotel? You heard Dima's instructions?"

With his face drained of all blood, Reed nodded. "Your brother was quite explicit in his instructions, Miss Rodchenko. He wanted it recorded on video so he could watch it later."

"Doesn't matter," Alina mumbled right before she tumbled unconscious to the van's floor. "I died a long time ago."

12

ALINA

ALINA WOKE IN A SHABBY ROOM, THE FLICKERING yellow ceiling light and the smell of borscht drifting under the door confirming she was still in Russia. Hearing the light play of fingertips over a keyboard, she rolled onto one side and saw the back of the man they called Reed.

Wearing a headset, he spoke into its microphone. "She's awake."

Covering the mouthpiece, he glanced over his shoulder and tossed a nod at the ice chest next to the bed. "Get yourself something to eat and drink."

She didn't care about food or water. Her thoughts were consumed with Bogdan—her son—and Mikhael, though she wished she could forget the big Russian.

Sitting up, she reached for one of the water bottles, discreetly testing its weight in case she needed to smack the American upside his head. At little more than sixteen wobbly ounces, she didn't think it would even momentarily stun him, so she cracked the seal on the cap and took a long drink.

Her voice squeaked like a rusty hinge when she spoke. "How long was I asleep?"

Maybe there was still time to undo the terrible mistake these men had made in trying to help her.

Reed lifted a single finger. She thought for a second he was signaling an hour, but that was too short.

A day was too long.

Realizing he was ordering her to silence, she shifted along the mattress until she could see his computer monitor. Like Bogdan's video games, green and red images moved on one half of the screen. Images from the night vision cameras filled the other half. An iPad was propped up next to him, its display showing thermal views.

"To your right, ten feet and closing," he said.

"What—what is this?" she demanded, jumping to her feet.

"Sit," he ordered, his voice like a steel dagger sheathed in the softest velvet. "You don't want me to make any mistakes on this. I assure you."

Her ass hit the mattress at the same time her mouth slammed shut. Her gaze scanned each image on the computer and tablet. One of the dots was neither red nor green—it was blue and represented a body far smaller than the rest that showed on the thermal, where another blue dot appeared over his head.

Bogdan—her son was that little blue dot and all the other people in the building, red or green, were armed and ready to kill.

"No, please," she croaked, but the American had blocked her voice out. His ears were attuned only to the communication stream from the headset and any movement she might make to stop him.

One of the red figures dropped and stopped moving. A green one stood almost directly over him. The red man offered one last jerk as a bullet entered his head and then the green man moved on.

Adrenaline flooded her blood. She lunged for the small wastebasket with the condoms and vodka bottles the last tenant had left behind and unloaded the contents of her stomach.

"Please, who is green?"

He didn't answer. Looking at the display again, she drew her own conclusions. The Rodchenko thugs were red because a red dot hovered over the man holding Bogdan. By his height and thin frame, she knew who hid behind her son's body—her half-brother.

Dima faced the door, one arm holding a gun, the other wrapped around Bogdan's neck. He had claimed the boy as his son, but that was a lie. He had never cared for him, only cared how he could use Alina's son to control and hurt her. The boy thought she was his aunt, Dima slowly warping Bogdan's opinion of her, allowing Alina to be in her son's presence only a few hours each month.

Now the coward was using the boy as a human shield.

A figure took up most of the thermal display on the iPad, its brightness and size blocking the reading for Dima and Bogdan.

"Straight from your shoulder, hold..." Reed said, all of his attention on the iPad. "Hold...hold...shoot!"

Alina screamed, the howl drawn out and turning her throat raw. The green figure dashed to the left of the screen. She could see another green figure kick in the door, but Dima was on the ground, unmoving, the blue figure covering him and also motionless.

The shooter entered the room and scooped Bogdan up. The boy started fighting, kicking and punching at the giant who held him. Fresh air filled Alina's lungs at the sight.

"Target acquired, pull back," Reed ordered. "All threats show as neutralized."

She scanned the screens again to see that Reed was right. The Rodchenko men were flat, dead or dying. One of the green men was slung over a team member's back, his vitals showing in a readout at the bottom of the screen.

Hurt but not dying.

13

ALINA

As soon as the operation to rescue Bogdan from Dima's safe house successfully concluded, Reed packed up his equipment and hustled Alina out to an old sedan. The American had given her no idea of where they were going, deferring her questions over and over with the promise someone would fill her in when they met up with Kane and Mikhael.

"We have no papers," she said as they drove out of Moscow. "Dima took control of our passports and visas after we cleared customs."

His mouth quirked and he strummed his fingers along the steering wheel. "Not every flight has to go through customs and immigration."

She lapsed into silence and wondered how Mikhael had come to have friends like Reed and Kane—and why he had let her languish all those years in misery when he had such means to rescue her.

The fault was hers—of course. Her entire life, the fault was always hers. She had treated him cruelly at their last meeting in New York. He couldn't know then, or even now, that it was to keep her father's men from killing him.

She might have risked everything that day in the library if only she had known that their one night together had put a baby in her womb. That painful knowledge came two months later.

Her first month of an absent period, she marked up to stress. It had happened before. The second missed period came with an inability to eat breakfast without throwing it up, something one of her father's staff noticed and reported to the old man.

That was the day her misery reached its flash point.

Seeing Reed tense at the wheel, she looked around for suspicious vehicles. When nothing caught her attention, she looked at the road side signs to read which city they were coming up on.

"Was the safe house in Novgorod?"

He nodded. "Rodchenko stashed your son there after Nazarov's solo attempt to kidnap you."

Slowly, she processed the information, focusing first on the memory of one of Dima's brigadiers swooping in like a vulture and grabbing the boy and a few bags as she begged in the hallway to go with them.

The man had punched her in the stomach to shut her up, in front of Bogdan, who watched emotionlessly, his life around his so-called father inuring him to violence, even when it was carried out against a woman who cherished every moment she was allowed to spend with him.

Her mind drifted to Mikhael and all the visible marks of what had happened to him after she had forced him yet again to flee from an attempt to rescue her. When her mind turned away from that memory, she realized what else Reed had said.

"What makes you think he's my son?"

His mouth curled up at the side she could see. "Beyond how long it took you to challenge my statement? I looked through the rest of the photos on your phone."

"I see." She didn't, not really. She also didn't know just how much Reed had pieced together. Let him think the boy was hers and Dima's. That was, after all, what Dima had told their father to keep the old man from beating her to death.

Yeah—for one moment only, her half-brother had seemed to play the hero. But he quickly proved no better than a cat choosing to keep its favorite mouse alive.

"You should rest," Reed suggested, one hand fiddling with the sedan's navigation system. "And eat."

Taking his sunglasses off, he handed them to her. "I

don't expect any trouble skirting Novgorod, but it's best you put these on and lower your seat. I'll wake you when we get to St. Petersburg."

Accepting his offer, she hooked his gaze for a moment. His face lit with a genuine smile, its tilt apologetic over the stress he had caused her in masterminding her kidnapping and Bogdan's rescue.

"I don't care about me," she said, voice breaking. "Just promise me my son is safe."

"I promise I'll do everything I can to keep him from harm."

Briefly, she touched his arm. It wasn't the pledge she had asked for, but it was the best she could hope for.

ALINA

FOUR HOURS LATER, IN THE SUITE OF AN AMERICAN hotel in St. Petersburg, with Reed still her only guard, Alina retreated into the bathroom. The drive, quiet and uneventful, had been anything but restful. These men who had rescued her and her son now controlled her as surely as Dima had.

She didn't know when she might see Bogdan, what the boy had been told, or what would happen next. The boy's birth certificate was a fiction her father had arranged, with Dima as the father and a dead woman as the mother.

DNA would prove her claim, but she needed a lawyer for that. And how could she get a lawyer when she legally owned nothing and would have the remaining members of the Rodchenko crime family and their allies hunting her down?

"Breathe," she warned herself in the bathroom mirror as she ran a washcloth under cold water.

She wrung the cloth out and pressed it to her cheeks, her gaze avoiding the mirror. She didn't need the visual reminder that she looked like shit. Dark circles hollowed out her eyes. Her face, neck and hands had taken on an ashen hue, as if she'd fallen very ill.

Pushing up her sleeves, she saw the same pallid grayness.

She would terrify Bogdan when he saw her!

Turning the faucet on, Alina let the sink fill with hot water. She stripped her blouse off, only her plain white bra covering her upper torso. She dipped a fresh wash cloth in the steaming water and began to scrub at her neck and face, the vigorous rubbing bringing a little color to her wan cheeks.

She moved on to her hands and arms, the skin unresponsive to the heat or rough scouring. Slapping at the drain lift, she tossed the wash cloth into the sink and turned in search of a towel.

Mikhael stood a few feet outside the open bathroom door. He held a loose square of folded clothing. His face was still a mottled mess of colors and swollen tissue.

Snatching a guest robe off the hook, she quickly shoved her arms in and tied the sash, but not before he had seen the scars that crisscrossed her body front and back.

He swallowed, his bruised and swollen lips parting momentarily before sealing again. Glaring at him, Alina stepped forward and snatched the clothes he had brought her. She spun, headed into the bathroom.

Mikhael hooked the sash where it ran along the back. Feeling the tug, she twisted and tried to stare him into releasing his hold. Grabbing more of the robe, he pulled her close, took the outfit away and placed it on the dresser.

His breathing grew harsh as he pushed one sleeve of the robe up as high as it would go. He rotated her arm, the thin, long scars visible front and back, top and bottom. He turned her so that she faced away from him, her eyes shutting with the humiliation of his inspection.

He tugged the robe down her back as she clutched at the front panels.

"Stop," she rasped, her voice as dry and gritty as used up sandpaper.

"No," he answered softly, turning her yet again and pulling her hands down to her sides so that he could inspect the scarring.

She watched his face, his expression collapsing as he studied how the scarring on her front side was concentrated around her stomach, the faded evidence of a potentially deadly beating older and deeper than the stretch marks from what he must realize was a pregnancy.

Bringing the edges of the robe together, he tied the sash for her.

"Bogdan," he started before his own bitter laugh interrupted him. "Dima dyed the boy's hair and brows black."

She said nothing, would not have this conversation with him—not when it was an interrogation, an accusation against her hanging in the air.

"When I finally peeled his teeth off my arm," Mikhael continued, "I thought I was looking into my mother's eyes. Same blue but with a white hot hate instead of Kata's cold indifference."

Alina wrapped her arms around herself and squeezed her eyes shut so hard the low rumble of tension from the straining muscles muffled his voice.

Gripping her elbows, he tugged her against him, her arms trapped between their bodies.

"Who tried to beat the baby out of you?"

She shook her head. She didn't want to remember the electrical cord in her father's hand, how he had stopped halfway through the ordeal to pull out a pocket knife and strip the protective rubber away at the end to expose the sharp copper wires.

It had taken years before she stopped reliving the attack in her nightmares. Not that her waking nightmares stopped. Dima had taken over, his abuse more constant but seldom physical.

She started to shake, her stomach grinding like small pebbles in a pool of acid because she'd already thrown up all she could.

"Let me get dressed."

"Who beat you here?" he growled, his hand leaving her elbow to curve around her stomach with a soft, cradling touch.

"Papa," Alina whispered and tried to pull away.

His hand slid behind her and settled against the curve of her back. "And here?"

"Papa at first. Dima after Papa died."

The old man had been beyond furious at her pregnancy. With Mikhael thought dead, he had immediately arranged to marry her off to a lesser family within the syndicate in an attempt to join territories. Finding her pregnant, he had turned insane in his rage, his hand stopped only by Dima's return and false claim of paternity.

Once she delivered the baby, the beatings resumed each time she was caught whispering into Bogdan's ear that she was his mother. The last time, when the boy was three and her father more than a year in his grave, Dima had almost beat her to death. After that, she was never left alone with her child and was blocked more and more from seeing him at all.

"Please," she bit out, her voice beginning to break. "Can I get dressed?"

Releasing his hold on her, Mikhael retrieved the clothes from the top of the dresser and handed them to her.

He left with a warning on his lips.

"We are not done talking, my Alina."

MIKHAEL

Mid-Flight – Over the Atlantic

THE BOY SAT NEAR THE REAR OF THE SMALL CHARTER plane, a set of headphones on as he watched a movie on Reed's computer, Reed in the seat next to him.

Several rows forward, Alina perched at the edge of her seat, her gaze never leaving the boy for more than a few seconds. Grabbing two water bottles from the galley, Nazarov stepped over her legs and plopped down next to her by the window.

They had not spoken since he had all but strip searched her in the bathroom. She had made sure to eliminate any opportunities for him to be alone with her again, locking a door if she went into a room, staying in it until she heard Kane or Reed's voice.

Without a word, he offered her the water. She took it absently, tucked it against her seat.

Beneath the yellow-tinged overhead lights, she looked like shit that had dried out in the sun. She wasn't eating, wasn't drinking—all because of him and the boy.

At first, the ten-year old had thrown himself into her arms, welcoming her tight, sobbing hug with one of his own. Pure joy had lit her face as she embraced her son, the same joy Nazarov had seen stamped in a wide grin on her morning visits to the bakery.

Then all hell broke loose when Bogdan pleaded with her to get him away from the bad men who had killed his papa and Alina tried to explain that the men in the room—Kane and Mikhael and Reed—had saved his life.

The boy had struck her with closed fists, called her all the names he had learned from the foul devil who had masqueraded as his father to keep Alina trapped and tormented in the Rodchenko family.

"Reed is watching him." Mikhael's tone, meant to coax her into relaxing, set her spine more stiffly against him. "Please, Alina, you're making yourself sick."

She choked on a laugh but collapsed back against her seat. Reaching across to where she had tucked the water bottle, he broke the seal, unscrewed the cap and pressed the bottle into her palm.

Swallowing roughly, she wiped at her cheek. He could tell by the tremble in her lips that raw emotions were sweeping through her, but he hadn't seen her shed a single tear since she had begged into the camera for his life.

He didn't know what to say, but he had to get her talking. Her mind was poisoning her body.

"Bogdan thinks I'm the monster who killed his father."

Her head bobbed. She stopped staring at the backrest in front of her and glanced at his hands as he gripped his knees.

"Were you the one who shot through the wall?"

"Yeah," he rasped, realizing his hands had started to shake. "I don't think I could have if..."

"If you had known Bogdan was yours."

"Yes."

He looked at her face but she kept her gaze trained away from his. This was the first time she had acknowledged what he already knew. The boy was his, the result of that one night of stolen bliss in a house filled with hate.

Part of him wanted to admonish her for not telling him before the raid. She'd had time and an opening before she lost consciousness, but she had intentionally withheld the information.

Why? To protect him or the boy?

"How are we getting back into the States?" she asked, distracting him from his own questions.

He looked at where Kane politely pretended to be asleep in his seat after spending the first half of the flight in the cockpit using a secure radio channel.

Answering, he nodded at the man. "As of half an hour ago, this is a U.S. diplomatic flight.

MIKHAEL

Undisclosed location - Virginia

BARS WERE INSTALLED ON THE WINDOWS OF ONE OF the bedrooms at the safe house Stark International provided Alina and Bogdan—not because of anyone the Rodchenko family might send to exact revenge but to keep the boy from running away. All three of the bedrooms opened onto the living room, where Mikhael slept on a couch that his big frame overflowed.

For added security, he installed a slide bolt on the outside of Bogdan's bedroom door.

A child psychiatrist visited three times a week during the first two weeks and advised them to tell Bogdan the truth about Alina being his mother and Mikhael his father. The boy had turned wild after they followed the advice, injuring the psychiatrist so that she hadn't returned in the two weeks since.

Whenever the boy exploded into one of his violent tantrums, Mikhael would wrap his arms and legs around Bogdan and hold tight until the child exhausted himself and could be safely locked in his room.

Alina watched both of them throughout the day with a haunted gaze, an apology delivered with each glance she cast in their direction. Mostly she looked like she was sorry she had ever been born.

She still refused to cry.

Mikhael waited, certain she would break, maybe so hard she could never be put back together—not by doctors or psychologists, and certainly not by him.

Sometimes she would answer one of his questions, usually after he had to wrestle with the boy and was almost as exhausted as Bogdan. Other times he eavesdropped on the answers she gave the FBI and U.S. District Attorney—but those answers didn't interest him so much.

In exchange for straightening out the birth certificate issues and giving her and Bogdan new identities, they wanted to know about the structure of the Rodchenko crime family. Who reported to whom, what were the rivalries within the organization, who were the weak links that might be turned and other things like that were of the greatest interest to the men who visited the house.

But every now and then her voice would hitch as she talked to the government agents and Mikhael would have a new question to ask her once the men left, like what happened two years after Mikhael disappeared when the old man died showing the same medical symptoms as Kata.

The one question he didn't have the guts to ask was whether she had only sent him away that day in the library because she was trying to save his life, sacrificing herself just as she had sacrificed over and over in the almost eleven years since then.

He didn't want to know that she had meant every word she said.

After all, he still loved her. Had never stopped loving her.

Turning on his side on the narrow couch, he sighed as he heard the distant approach of a storm. The safe house was east of Richmond and a bit more than a hundred miles south of Arlington where his job and a house he'd bought after leaving his last employer waited for him.

He hadn't gotten the all clear yet on returning to work—at least if he wanted to make regular visits to the safe house. He expected clearance soon. Dima had been universally hated and his death had created a power vacuum that others within the organization were too busy trying to fill to take time out to avenge their Pakhan's death—or even investigate it, especially given the precision and heavy tactical support with which the assassination had occurred.

The sky growled a little more loudly. Hurricane season with a slow one moving up the coast. There was too much distance between the safe house and the ocean to worry about the direct effects, but tornados were becoming more of a problem.

Picking his smartphone up from the coffee table and checking his weather app, he wondered whether storms still terrified Alina. They hadn't had one in the month they'd been in the safe house, at least not a real one with heavy thunder and lightning and a swirling threat that the Hand of God was about to pluck entire families out of the sky and fling them back to the ground.

Hearing the creak of Alina's closet door, he sat up. It creaked a second time and then the door handle clicked shut right before the curtains at the front door gently glowed for a second.

Resting his elbows on his knees, he planted his face against his palms and concentrated. He listened to the storm grow closer and for signs that Alina or Bogdan needed him.

He didn't expect the thunder or lightning to wake the boy. His tantrums wore him out, often causing him to sleep upwards of ten hours after he finally went limp. It was Alina he worried about, as fragile and silent as she had been rendered by everything that had happened in Russia and Bogdan's reaction to finding out she was his mother.

She didn't need the weather to turn furious on top of everything else.

A loud crack of thunder pulled him onto his feet. He padded softly over to her shut bedroom door, the lesser grumblings of the storm masking the groans of the old wooden floor. He leaned in, listened for any sound of distress.

Hearing muffled whimpers, he eased the door open as lightning flashed to reveal an empty bed. Thunder boomed and she whimpered again, the noise leading him to her closet.

"Alina," he whispered as he opened the door.

At first, he saw nothing. The floor was pitch black, no sign of her pale skin or arms. He reached down, his hand colliding with a blanket and, beneath that, the top of her head. Slowly, he drew the fabric away to expose her face.

"Come out of there, baby," he said before he could stop the endearment from escaping.

He had promised himself he wouldn't wear his heart on his sleeve around her. She didn't need the added pressure. Shaking her head, she tugged the blanket out of his hand and whipped it back over her head.

Getting on his hands and knees, Mikhael elbowed his way into the closet, crowding her at first then pulling her onto his lap.

"You don't have to face the storms alone anymore," he coaxed as she trembled stiffly in his embrace. "Not if you don't want to."

"Go, please." Her tone turned robotic as it did whenever he or one of the men from the government asked her questions. "It's embarrassing to have anyone see me like this."

Ignoring her request, he rubbed at her forearms in an attempt to soothe her. His hand encountering a wet spot on her flesh, he traced a circle, the pad of his finger picking up small, even indentations.

"Why do you bite yourself?"

She laughed and it pained him that it was as bitter as all the other laughs that had escaped her lips since he had entered the bakery in Moscow.

"Because if I don't bite myself, I'll scream, and I don't want the microphones to hear me."

His arms tightened around her. "There are no microphones here, baby. Kane wouldn't lie to me and I won't lie to you."

She exhaled, slow and unconvinced.

"There were microphones in Papa's shed. Cameras, too. Dima had them installed. Do you remember the year they put on the metal roof?"

Mikhael forced his body to relax so he wouldn't crush her in his embrace. "Someone put you in the garden shed during a storm?"

"Every storm," she answered. "After Papa died. Me

in my nightgown, hauled from bed, not even a robe. Night vision cameras so Dima could watch..."

Rage boiled inside him. What had he done, leaving her there?

"He wanted to marry me, you know? Said I could be Bogdan's stepmother..."

Bile coated Mikhael's tongue. He couldn't take her voice any longer, the catatonic monotone. Forcing her to turn in his arms, he pressed her face against his chest and shushed her. When the thunder shook the windows, it was his flesh she bit into, over and over until the storm finally rolled past and they fell asleep on the floor of her closet, her body still cradled against his.

MIKHAEL

ALINA'S PANICKED SCREAM WOKE MIKHAEL. HIS ARMS grasped at nothing. The boy shouted, his voice twisting like a rabid animal as Mikhael lumbered out of the closet on deadened limbs.

Bitch!

With no other voices reaching his ears, Mikhael knew Bogdan was speaking to his mother. Flinging open the bedroom door, he looked immediately toward the kitchen where Alina was trying to keep the boy at arm's length and away from sharper instruments as Bogdan wielded a fork.

A patch of blood stained the forearm of her plain white nightgown from where Bogdan had already stabbed her. More vile words and accusations spewed from the child's mouth. She was a bitch, a filthy whore who had seduced Mikhael into murdering his papa.

With shaking hands, he stepped silently behind Bogdan, cupped beneath each armpit and lifted the boy off his feet, spinning at the same time so that there was only empty air to kick at and not his mother's face.

"Drop the fork," he ordered coldly.

Bogdan tightened his grip on the utensil. "Fuck you!"

Just as quickly as he had scooped the boy up, he dropped him and grabbed both wrists separately. Ignoring Bogdan's thrashing, Mikhael squeezed at the pressure points on each side of the boy's wrist. Twisting like a demon, Bogdan tried to find a patch of Mikhael's skin to bite, but the big man held him taut, his arms stretched as far as they would go without dislocating Bogdan's shoulders.

"Please, don't hurt him," Alina pleaded, stepping toward them and reaching for the fork.

"Stay back," Mikhael bellowed as the boy tried to twist his hand and aim the sharp tines of the fork in Alina's direction. He squeezed a little harder at the pressure points, but only managed to make the boy growl furiously.

A rough chuckle escaped Mikhael. He had finally found one point on which the boy was nothing like Dima. He didn't roll belly up at the first bit of pain.

"You know how this ends," he thundered in the boy's ear. "Let go."

The scent of shoe polish filled Mikhael's nostrils as

he straightened. Looking more closely at Bogdan, he saw that the boy had applied the substance to the blond roots on his scalp and his eyebrows.

Alina caught the direction of Mikhael's gaze. "He was knocking at his door, said he had to go the bathroom—he must have hid the polish in his room yesterday. I was going to wash it before you woke up..."

"Filthy whore!" the boy shouted. "You know papa hates it when it's yellow!"

Patience hanging by a thread, Mikhael squeezed the pressure points one last time and the fork clattered to the ground. Wrapping his arms around the boy's chest, he sat on a kitchen chair.

"You stabbed your mother," he said, the low, flat tone filled with menace.

"He didn't mean—"

Mikhael shot her objection down with a sharp glance.

"Show him your arms."

She shook her head. His meaning was clear. He had said "arms," not "arm." He wanted the boy to see not only the damage from the fork but all the scars that crisscrossed from a few inches above her wrist up past her biceps.

Kneeling on the floor, she tried to placate Bogdan. "Let me wash the polish out, it's not healthy. We'll get some proper dye at the store."

Seeing the boy's cheeks hollow, Mikhael nipped at

his ear. "Don't think about spitting at anyone, especially her."

With memories of Osip and Kostya spitting on his bruised and bloody face surfacing, Mikhael squeezed the boy a little harder.

"No dye," he ground out. "Bring me my clippers."

Alina's face went hard. "No. You are not going to shave him."

The boy went wild as understanding finally sank in.

Ignoring both of their protests, Mikhael stood, the boy helpless in his arms, and went into the bathroom. He shut the door and braced his back against it so Alina could not intervene beyond pounding her fists raw on the wooden surface.

One arm pinning the boy to his chest, he turned the clippers on and ran a line up and over the boy's scalp. As the black hair fell around Bogdan's shoulders, the boy went limp. Still blocking the door with his weight, Mikhael angled his body to see the boy's face.

The stark blue eyes were open, the jaw slack.

"I'm sorry, my son," Mikhael whispered, hoping the boy was just playing possum and not in a deep state of shock as the last vestiges of his Rodchenko past drifted to the floor.

MIKHAEL

THE DAY DIDN'T GET ANY BETTER. BOGDAN REMAINED unmoving after Mikhael finished shaving the boy's hair at the clipper's closest setting and washed the shoe polish off what remained.

Carrying Bogdan into the front room, he placed him on the couch, across from where Alina sat in a side chair, her arm awkwardly held to avoid getting blood from her sleeve on the fabric. Turning his back on Bogdan, Mikhael knelt in front of her.

He reached for the cuff of her gown. She recoiled and pulled the arm closer to her body. Her haunted gazed darted in his direction then away just as quickly.

"It needs disinfected and bandaged," he said, settling onto the floor in defeat. "If you won't let me take care of it, you need to."

Careful not to come into contact with him, she eased out of the chair and went into the bathroom.

With a quick glance at the boy to make sure he hadn't moved, Mikhael rose and went into the kitchen. He would need locks for some of the kitchen drawers and cabinets to secure anything the boy might turn into a weapon—which was pretty much everything. Pulling out his phone, he started dictating a list into his texting app.

After a lifetime under the thumb of the Rodchenko family's hired thugs, Alina hadn't wanted guards outside or in the house. A security team was still in place in another house across the street. If he hadn't insisted on removing the listening devices and cameras discreetly placed around the safe house, the team would have been able to stop the boy before he had stabbed her with the fork.

Sighing, he hit send, requesting one of the team members across the street to pick up the supplies. No more glass or china, just plastic, plus brackets and combination locks to lock up the necessary dangers.

He hoped the boy hadn't picked up Dima's fascination with fire.

A shudder passed through him as he remembered the long ago arson that happened in the days following his ejection from the Rodchenko family. He saw the building filled with families, their lives acceptable collateral damage so long as it meant Mikhael Nazarov died that night.

And he had died—inside at least. Making the jump between the burning building and the next one, running like a rat to disappear into the night. Two hours later and an hour out of the city, he had contacted the FBI agent whose assassination he had heard Dmitrey Rodchenko plotting.

That one call for help had snowballed into rushed training for a spot on a joint task force, his age, coloring and Moscow accent matching a low level dead Russian convict whose identity they could steal and use to insert him into the Volkov family.

He saved lives with the work he did in Russia—took more than a few, as well. But the work he did for the task force and then for security companies like Stark International never made him feel alive for more than a few minutes at a time.

Each night, he crawled into bed and woke up a corpse.

Dragging himself up out of the past, he saw Alina slip into the kitchen and begin to fix breakfast. Dressed, with her face washed and her long, black hair pulled into a tight knot, she kept her head down. Whenever Mikhael moved the slightest, she froze in place.

She was never going to forgive him. Not for what he had just done—not even for saving her in Moscow and rescuing the boy from Dima. She couldn't see past the boy's current frame of mind. He had been happy before Mikhael's arrival, now he was miserable. That was all she could focus on. That and the boy's glaring hate for her.

Going into the attached living room, Mikhael sat at the opposite end of the couch from his son. The boy looked at the blank television screen while Mikhael's attention floated between Bogdan and Alina.

She made oatmeal and buttered toast and marmalade, something that didn't require trusting Bogdan with a fork again. Ignoring her own needs, she brought a tray to Mikhael then returned with a second tray and knelt in front of the boy. She tried to coax him into taking a piece of toast. When he remained limp and unblinking, she held the bowl in one hand and scooped up some of the oatmeal.

"Try to eat a little, *malcheek*," she urged, the spoon hovering an inch from his mouth.

With no time to react, Mikhael saw the boy's face suddenly narrow. Bogdan's arm whipped toward the bowl and made contact, plastering the hot oatmeal against Alina's blouse and drawing a pained gasp from her lips.

"Perhaps the psychiatrist—" she started.

"No." Mikhael winced at the harsh tone with which he answered, but he knew what Alina didn't know. After the earlier displays of violence, the doctor had wanted to drug and institutionalize the boy "for a few months or more."

"Go see to yourself," he ordered, settling back against the couch and taking a bite of his toast. "I will watch him."

She looked at Bogdan and then the bits of oatmeal that had missed her clothing and landed on the floor. Cupping her hand, she started to scrape the mess on the carpet in one direction.

"I said take care of yourself," Mikhael repeated, the already hard edge to his voice growing sharper. "He will take care of the mess when he finally gets hungry enough to behave."

MIKHAEL

BY FOUR IN THE AFTERNOON, THE BOY'S STOMACH WAS growling loud enough for both of his parents to hear. Disobeying Mikhael's order, Alina placed a peanut butter and jelly sandwich on a paper plate and left it on the coffee table, a plastic cup with milk resting next to it.

Her gaze beseeched Mikhael to turn on the television and distract the boy with one of his favorite shows. He ignored the pleas in her eyes and, six hours later, the food and drink remained untouched.

"He has to drink something," she whispered, approaching Mikhael for the first time since she had brought him breakfast.

"So do you," he countered. "Go to bed. I'll get him to drink something."

Seeing the shadow that crossed her face, his mouth

drew into a deep scowl.

"For the love of God, Alina, I'm not going to water-board him!"

She blinked, but her eyes were dry. No more crying for Alina. No more smiling either.

"Get ready for bed," he ordered as he began to chew over what needed to be done.

The boy took his catharsis with violent tantrums. Alina allowed herself no release at all. No tears, no raised voice, no angry shaking of her hands. Every day, she faded a little bit more.

Sitting in silence with Bogdan, he watched Alina disappear into the bedroom. She shut the door. He heard the slide of the dresser drawer and closed his eyes. He imagined her body, the marks across her back from the electrical cord beatings, the same network of abuse on her legs and arms.

"Maybe if I sit with him," Alina suggested after she opened her door.

Mikhael nodded at her bed. "I'll bring him in a few minutes."

Another flicker of mistrust crossed her face but she turned back into the room and sat on the edge of the mattress. Mikhael picked the boy up, but took him into the bathroom. Leaving the door open, he stood Bogdan in front of the toilet and turned the water on at a barely audible trickle.

The boy shot him a dirty look, the sour twist of his

mouth indicating he knew what Mikhael was up to.

"I can wait all night," Mikhael said as he turned his back on the boy and blocked the doorway. "I'm not going to have you wet yourself when you throw your next tantrum."

Not that the boy had done so already. But he hadn't urinated since at least early morning. And a tantrum was imminent because Mikhael planned on triggering it. He wasn't going to watch the woman he loved wither away and his son continue turning to stone until one day the boy realized with a devastating clarity just how much pain he had inflicted on his mother and how much she had already suffered to protect him.

The sound of water running in the sink was joined by liquid hitting the toilet bowl. Mikhael suppressed a grin and kept his back turned until a few seconds after the boy flushed.

He had to fight to keep the smile from his face as he turned to Bogdan and maneuvered the uncooperative pile of flesh over to the sink. He squirted soap on the boy's hands then waited several long seconds before the kid shot Mikhael another furious look then shoved his hands under the faucet and washed them on his own.

Two wins in his column, Mikhael mused as he turned off the water and dried Bogdan's limp hands. Pretty much his only wins as far as Alina and the boy were concerned. But hopefully there would be more before the night was through.

Placing a firm hand against Bogdan's shoulder blade, he tried to coax the boy out of the room. The little mule's legs locked straight so that any pressure threatened to propel him face first into the floor.

Fine—carrying him wasn't a loss even though Bogdan seemed to think so.

"You know what I remember about your Papa," he asked softly as he carried his son toward Alina's bedroom.

Hearing the question, her head whipped up.

Mikhael warned her to stay silent with a narrowing of his gaze.

"He loved the mafia movies, Godfather, Wise Guys, anything with a lot of bang, bang, BOOM."

The boy looked uncomfortably inward as the volume of Mikhael's words grew. Ignoring how Bogdan stiffened in his arms, the big Russian sat in the dainty reading chair shoved in one corner of Alina's bedroom.

Worry clouding her gaze, Alina swiveled a few degrees to stare hopefully at her son.

"Roll up your sleeves," Mikhael demanded of her, his arm looped around Bogdan so the boy couldn't bolt.

"You know I won't." Her gaze hit the floor then skittered around the room like a cornered animal looking for escape. When she finally looked up, she nailed Mikhael with a hard stare. "He's as much a victim as we are."

Mikhael shook his head. "No. And he never will be.

Now show him your arms."

Her body slumped in passive disobedience as Mikhael continued to hammer at her.

"He stabbed you today. Maybe next time he'll get a knife when we have our backs turned."

"He won't" she protested, ignoring the boy's satisfied huff at the scenario Mikhael had just laid out. "He was upset because Dima could be cruel when the blond started to show."

She dipped her head, tried to catch Bogdan's attention. "Your uncle didn't like your hair looking like your real papa's."

"Lying whore," the boy muttered.

Forcing his arms not to squeeze a little respect and a lot of sense into Bogdan, Mikhael changed arguments with the woman.

"There are only two paths that lead out from where you want to go, my Alina," he started, the soft voice eerily ominous. "The first path, he never, ever accepts you."

Her breathing hitched, but her face remained placid, her eyes as dry as sun baked clay.

"He never accepts you," Mikhael pressed on, "and he keeps on hurting you physically and emotionally."

Another satisfied huff from the boy made Mikhael want to rap the kid on his nose. Maybe it was already too late. The Rodchenkos taught their children to fear and hate from the cradle. Sweet Alina had somehow escaped that curse, only in part because her early years had been spent in a place slightly less horrible than living daily in her father's presence.

Mashing and rolling his lips, Mikhael hesitated to say anything more. Maybe waiting a few days was best. Maybe medication like the doctor had said—something to calm the boy.

A second away from Mikhael relenting, Alina met his gaze with a questioning look.

He closed his eyes, not wanting to see the pain he was about to inflict scratch and claw its way across her beautiful face.

"Then there's the second path. The second path, he realizes too late and he can no longer accept himself. He takes all the hate he has shown you and turns it on himself."

The boy started to twist angrily in his arms. "Shut up, stupid. I hate you! I hate you both! She is not even a Rodchenko. My papa said so."

"Alina, show him what they did to your arms, your papa and his," Mikhael said then, firmly but gently. "He needs to see it."

After a moment's hesitation, slowly, she pushed one sleeve up.

The boy wouldn't look, so Mikhael wrapped one big hand around the top of his skull and forced his gaze up.

"Both sleeves," he said when the boy remained

stubbornly stiff and unresponsive.

Fresh hurt unfurled in her dark gaze as she stared at her son's face and worked the second sleeve up to her elbow.

"Your papa and his papa did that," Mikhael told the boy.

"She was being bad so they had to discipline her," Bogdan accused. "Papa told me she was a filthy whore who was always bad. That's why I always hated her, because I'm a good boy."

Mikhael watched Alina flinch at the last statement, but remain otherwise expressionless throughout the torrent of hateful words that spewed from Bogdan's mouth. She'd had ten years of this, ten years of training in how to take this kind of torture without reacting.

Mikhael had no such training, no such patience when it came to the woman he loved suffering in silence. "You say you always hated her. But she has always loved you, Bogdan. Your entire life."

"I. Don't. Care!" the boy screamed, straining against Mikhael's hard grip, his slender body leaning toward Alina. "Those are her fault, not mine! You can't make me feel bad for her!"

Head drooping, Alina quickly started to push her sleeves back down.

Growling, Mikhael stood and dumped the boy in the chair. A soft kick closed the bedroom door and then his arm shot out to lock it.

Slowly he stalked toward the bed and murmured softly to Alina, "Come here, love."

Alina looked up, the first threat of tears making her eyes shimmer.

So damn beautiful and hurting so badly, all because of his mistakes all those years ago.

It ends tonight.

Bending down, he lifted the hem of her long nightgown up to her knees.

"They did this to her, too," he told the boy before straightening and pointing at the headboard a second time. "Turn around, Alina. He needs to see your back."

"Please, no," she whisper-cried.

Her shoulders shook with the kind of bone-deep distress and anguish bred from years of mental torment.

Mikhael waited for her to comply, wanting only to help her, not break her.

He knew the moment she realized he would not relent tonight, and just like that, all the fight was gone from her.

She let him turn her and unbutton the back of the nightgown, expose the scars that her son has never seen.

Returning to the chair, Mikhael lifted the mulish boy out if it and stood him a foot away from Alina. He secured his hands on both sides of Bogdan's head so he couldn't look away. "Do you see the scars your mother has hidden from you?"

"It looks like someone took a giant cheese grater to your back," Bogdan said callously, sounding like a robotic clone of the little devil himself. Despite his cold words, the young boy couldn't completely mask the look of horror on his face at what he was seeing.

A harsh cry wrenched Alina's throat. She rolled across the mattress until she faced the opposite wall, her back still exposed, her entire body shuddering with pained tears.

"Say what you want," Mikhael growled and dragged the boy toward the bed. "But you will look at her. You will see what she has endured for you."

"No," the boy protested, his voice sounding weak for the first time tonight. "It hurts my eyes."

"It's your papa's work," Mikhael explained, holding the boy's chin so Bogdan couldn't look away again.

"She must have done something bad to deserve it," the boy maintained stubbornly, even as his eyes began filling with tears.

Drawing a long, slow breath, Mikhael fought the angry fire building inside him.

He's just a child, he reminded himself, a child mentally manipulated by a sociopath whose entire goal was to intentionally poison Bogdan against his own mother, just as Dmitrey had slowly poisoned Mikhael's mother against him.

Fueled by that memory, he pushed Bogdan closer, pointed out each scar marring Alina's flesh. "These were her punishment for loving you. But she never stopped. Every night she whispered to you when you were a baby, *'I am your mama, lubimi, know me. Know your mother loves you.'* And every night they punished her for that."

The first full-bodied sob tore through Alina's throat.

A matching one slipped past Bogdan's lips.

"You were lied to, Bogdan. Those marks across the front of her arms—the reason she wears long sleeves every day—are from when she shielded her belly so your grandfather couldn't beat you in her womb." Mikhael's voice went as cold as the boy's brainwashed soul as he pushed even more. "The marks on the other side of her arms are where she shielded her head from getting whipped and kicked so she wouldn't die with you in her belly."

One hand leaving Bogdan's head, Mikhael traced one of the scars that ran the full width of Alina's back. "She nearly didn't survive when she got this scar," Mikhael said, almost unable to speak those words out loud. But he kept going. He was getting through to Bogdan, he could feel it. "It was the last time she was able to hold you before your precious papa took you completely away from her and poisoned your mind with lies."

Alina's sobbing became uncontrollable. "Stop. Just stop." Her fingers curled around her ear, the nails denting the thin flesh and threatening to tear it.

But Mikhael couldn't stop. Not until this was over. Bogdan would not hurt Alina any more. "Your papa punished your mother for loving you. And now, you're doing your papa's work for him. *You* are hurting your mama, Bogdan. When all she has done is love and protect you."

Finally, Bogdan's legs gave out.

Mikhael let him crumple to his knees, his own stomach churning from what he had done, what he'd had to do.

The boy's frame shook with the tears he cried, just as Alina shook. Mikhael crawled onto the bed and tried to fasten her gown back in place, his deep voice attempting to soothe her but unable to do so as her dry heaves continued to shake her frame.

"Mama..."

The single word was no louder than a tearful whisper from Bogdan on the floor, but it froze Mikhael's hand.

"Mama," the boy repeated, a little louder, his voice sounding confused and grief-stricken.

Immediately, Mikhael got off the bed and crouched over the boy. Both mother and son were rocking themselves to find comfort, both inexperienced in finding comfort from others.

"Mama," the boy cried out in anguish as he watched —and truly saw for the first time—his mother's pain.

At the start of his broken sobbing, Alina quickly

rolled across the bed and reached with one shaking hand to brush her fingers lightly across the boy's nearly bald scalp.

With a hiccup, Bogdan looked up.

As soon as he did, she withdrew her hand, clearly unsure if the boy wanted her touching him at all.

Knowing that Bogdan wouldn't know how to convince Alina otherwise, Mikhael gently helped the boy onto his feet then lifted him onto the bed.

Exhausted, the boy instantly curled his body against Alina's and laid his head on her chest.

Mikhael's strained, pummeled heart constricted behind his ribcage when Alina tentatively curled an arm around him before cupping the boy's cheek tenderly.

With that, Mikhael returned to the chair, watching the two of them lay unmoving like that for several long minutes.

As Bogdan slowly fell asleep in his mother's arms, it didn't escape Mikhael's attention that Alina's eyes remained almost glassy, unfocused the entire time. And aside from the arm she kept around the boy's shoulders and the hand stroking his cheek, the rest of her was stiff, seemingly…disconnected.

The revelation was a crushing blow.

Mikhael had succeeded in finally giving Alina what she's always wanted—but the distant look on her face told him it came too late.

20

MIKHAEL

MIKHAEL WOKE WITH THE EXPECTATION THAT THE BOY might return to being unmanageable. But neither Bogdan nor Alina changed from how they had fallen asleep—the boy finally accepting Alina as his mother and Alina slowly closing herself off from all emotion.

On the third day following Bogdan's meltdown, Alina approached Mikhael after she had washed the breakfast dishes. She told him that she was moving her things to the third, and smallest, bedroom and Mikhael should stop sleeping on the couch and take the room she had previously used.

He tried to argue it, said he would take the smaller bedroom and that, for the boy's sake, it was best not to make any big changes, like shuttling her off to a room barely bigger than a walk-in closet. But by noon, she had moved her few possessions into the room and hauled the suitcase Mikhael had been living from into the master bedroom.

She started pushing the food around her plate at each meal, apologizing absently that it was too hot or too cold, too spicy or too bland. When he or the boy assured her it was fine, marvelous even, she said nothing more and put her fork down, motionless until she saw that they were done eating and she could begin clearing the table.

Too late, too late.

The words twisted through Mikhael's chest.

A few days later, when Bogdan fell asleep earlier than usual, he carried the boy to bed then cornered Alina.

"We need to talk."

Wiping her palms against her skirt, she nodded. When Mikhael stalled over where to start, she began.

"You said we're safe for now? That we don't have to stick so close to the house or worry about being seen?"

"Yes." He answered slowly, uncertain where she was headed with her questions.

"You can go back to your friends in Arlington?"

Fresh panic building in his chest, Mikhael didn't answer. She wanted him to leave.

Before he could ask her if that was what she wanted, she drew a deep breath then rocked him back on his heels with what she said next.

"I don't know that I can support him. I only have a

high school diploma and they never let me work. I was supposed to be someone's wife, then I couldn't even be that. It is best if you raise him."

"No," Mikhael said, reaching for her.

She tried to slip past him. He wrapped his hands around her elbows and she froze, her gaze locked off to the side.

"I will make sure you have all the money you need to take care of my son and..."

He wanted to say "my woman." That's what she would always be to him, even if he could never hold her again or kiss the lips that had grown flat and thin with her grief the past few weeks.

"You won't need to earn any money," he finished. "I know he said some cruel things—"

She shook her head violently, her chest shuddering with the need to unleash the tears building in her dark gaze. "He spoke the truth."

"No." Releasing her arms, Mikhael cupped her cheeks. "Where is my Alina."

A fat tear escaped each eye to run down her cheeks.

"I was never your Alina," she whispered. "I was just the girl you got pregnant."

His hands dropped away to clench at his sides. He wanted to smash a fist through the wall next to her. Instead he placed his palms flat against the paneling on either side of her.

"I shouldn't have sent you away like I did that night. I should have told you how much I loved you."

Every word coming out of his mouth seemed to make her shrink a little more. She was closing herself off, disappearing like some kind of magic folding box.

"We need to get out of this house," he said, pulling back. "There's a farm halfway between here and Arlington. It's a special place, part of a foundation that helps children coming from war zones to the U.S. for medical treatment. My boss's sister runs it…"

He trailed off when she said nothing.

"Reed is supposed to be there this week and you can meet Vivian, that's Stark's sister. She's a good listener."

"Take the boy. He likes your friend Reed."

She was back to her flat, robotic monotone. He wasn't even sure if she merely meant take Bogdan to the farm for a day while leaving her behind or take him forever. His gut told him it was probably the latter—she hadn't even said Bogdan's name.

"We'll all go tomorrow, after breakfast."

Fighting not to choke on his words, he brushed a strand of hair away from her face. She was fading in front of his eyes, but she was still the most beautiful woman he could imagine. He wanted to tell her that, but her ears were still flooded with everything the boy had said.

Stupid, fat, ugly, whore, cheese grater skin…

"Alina," he started, his throat locking up. He sucked a ragged breath in and stroked his thumb across her collarbone. "I am so sorry I pushed him...that he said—"

She brushed his hand away and turned toward her bedroom door. "If we're visiting your friends, there's ironing to do. Hang your clothes on the knob. I'll take care of them after I finish the boy's."

Without another word or a glance back, she disappeared into her room.

MIKHAEL

AFTER A MONTH COOPED UP IN THE SAFE HOUSE, Bogdan spent the drive to the farm with his nose pressed against the window. He produced a running commentary: a log truck, another log truck, Florida plates, New York plates...

Mikhael worried the New York plates might remind the boy of what he had lost from his old life, but Alina had assured Mikhael in the early weeks of staying at the safe house that Bogdan had been home schooled, with guards and cleaning staff his only playmates. Hell, Alina figured that Mikhael had already spent as much time around Bogdan as Dima had during the boy's first five years. After another month, she had said with a frown, Mikhael would be more than caught up.

"What did I say about seatbelts?" Mikhael warned as Bogdan released the catch on his device.

The boy slid across the seat to Mikhael's side, pulled the safety belt across his thin chest, and secured it before plastering his face against the window.

"Are there animals at the farm?"

"Milking goats, geese, chickens…" Mikhael confirmed. "There's a lake for fishing, too."

Straining forward, Bogdan put his hand on Mikhael's shoulder.

"I don't know how to fish," the boy said, a touch of entreaty in his tone.

"We'll learn together, then," Mikhael said, his gaze bouncing off Alina. "But maybe not today."

Alina was tucked against the door. Her eyes were open, but he doubted that she really saw anything. He couldn't even be sure she was following the conversation.

"This is it," he said, pulling the sedan up to a security gate.

A guard exited the building attached to the stone wall. With Stark International providing all the security, the man knew Mikhael by sight, but he still checked everyone in the vehicle and looked in the trunk before waving them through.

Having privately brainstormed the "Alina issue" with Reed and Vivian, he knew the two of them would be waiting in the resource center. He parked the sedan, gestured to Bogdan that he could get out, then went around to Alina's side and opened her door.

Her mouth danced with indecision.

"You can't stay in the car, my Alina."

When she still hesitated, he jutted his chin in Bogdan's direction and whispered. "He needs us to lead by example. You have to be open to leaving the cage you lived in for so long. It was his cage, too."

Gaze cast toward the ground, she unfolded herself from the car. Bogdan ran over and slid his hand against hers.

"It's just a few hours," Mikhael said, gesturing at the entrance. "You've endured far worse for far longer."

It was mean to say and he regretted it even as the words left his mouth, but it got her to move, the first step a rough jerk forward before she took up a smooth rhythm.

Entering the large, open workspace, Bogdan spotted Henley and launched himself at the man.

"Reed!"

Laughing, Reed caught the boy, spun him in a circle then placed him on his feet before turning to Mikhael and, beyond him, where she hung back near the door, Alina.

"Vivian is dealing with a travel visa issue that popped up," Reed said. "She'll be back any minute."

Mikhael glanced over his shoulder at Alina then returned his gaze to Reed. His brows lifted expectantly. He had texted Reed and Vivian the night before, after Alina had gone to bed. He needed Reed to keep

Bogdan occupied and Vivian to hopefully work some kind of magic with Alina. The woman definitely had some hard won skills in that respect. She had suffered her own trauma and had dedicated the last five years to helping others move past theirs.

Hopefully, his idea would not blow up in his face —again.

"Hey, champ," Reed said, taking Mikhael's subtle hint. "I just installed a flight simulator on my computer, want to try it out?"

The boy started to launch himself at Reed a second time but he pulled up short, spun and looked up at Mikhael. "Can I?"

Mikhael answered with a lift of his chin, the simple response and Reed's offer making the boy break into a wide grin.

Alone with Alina, Mikhael gestured at the big table in the center of the room where Vivian liked to do her intake briefings with the families her foundation housed while the children received medical care.

"Come sit."

As Alina slowly complied, her gaze slid over the table's surface. There were brochures for schools, information packets on education grants, tips for writing resumes and interviewing.

"What is this?" Alina asked, her voice thin with suspicion.

"Work, I guess," he answered, relieved that there

were multiple copies of everything so that it didn't look like the table was set with an agenda that revolved around Alina.

Circling the table, she took a seat opposite of where she had left him standing.

"Teddy bear!" Vivian Lodge squealed as she entered at the opposite side of the room. Breezing over to him so fluidly she could have been wearing skates, she wrapped her arms around him and squeezed for everything she was worth.

When she pulled back, there was a soft sheen of tears in her eyes.

"I just met your little guy, but he and Reed barely said so much as 'hello' because their noses were buried in a computer."

Laughing, she rolled her eyes and turned in Alina's direction.

"You must be…" Vivian started but then her voice caught.

Mikhael's balls shriveled up into his stomach, maybe even his throat because a lump had formed there just as quickly. It was a long shot, but he was counting on Vivian to put Alina at ease, to work her charms like she did with the refugees who came to the foundation, getting them to open up and, particularly the women, make the most of what was available during their stay.

So why the hell couldn't she say anything to Alina?

"This is Alina," Mikhael said, burying the growl in his voice beneath a cough. "Bogdan's mother."

Vivian nodded while Alina stared through both of them.

This was going to be a disaster.

All because he couldn't stop pushing.

"I hope I didn't just come off as rude," Vivian said, navigating her way around the table to where Alina sat. Perching on the edge of the table, she leaned down and captured Alina's hands. "But you seem so sad, it stunned me."

Alina's gaze darted to Mikhael. For days she had asked him for nothing, not for herself. Now her hollowed eyes were pleading for him to intervene, to let her leave and find someplace to hide until his visit was over.

Slowly, his heart knotting around itself, he shook his head. He would not intervene.

Releasing Alina's hands, Vivian reached for one of the brochures. "I'm used to working with foreigners, but you're American, yes? New York City?"

Alina's only answer was a hardened stare.

"My brother Collin says I'm a bit of a steamroller, and not as any kind of a compliment," Vivian confessed, looking down at the brochure with its picture of a happy college graduate. "But I have had to put my life back together. My husband died in front of me, a bullet through his head."

Alina's lips parted then bobbed for a second before her mouth snapped shut.

"This," Vivian said, her hand sweeping toward all the brochures and guidance packets, "is for another day, I think. Today…"

There was a long, uncomfortable pause as Vivian got ready to step off a very high cliff.

"Today, I'd like to do some fashion therapy."

Alina's gaze cut through the woman. Vivian Lodge was tall, thin but with a hidden strength. She wore a red silk shirt for the meeting and a long pencil skirt that reached halfway down her calves. Her nails were manicured, her hair professionally styled and colored to a light caramel.

Mikhael took a step forward to intervene. Vivian stepped in front of him. She wasn't capable of blocking out a man his size, but she had Alina's attention.

"Make-up, hair, clothes—"

"I need to stay in these clothes," Alina snapped.

Vivian softly pushed back at Alina's rejection. "There's still make-up and hair."

Before Alina could object again, Mikhael interrupted. "You need something to do while Bogdan visits with Reed. Go and make your host happy."

It was a low blow, making Alina feel like a bad guest. He had already done so many things to make her feel bad or to cause others to make her feel that way. But Alina needed the time with Vivian, to let the woman pamper her. Alina needed to be reminded of how beautiful she was, not just on the outside but even more so in her heart.

Politely waving Vivian away, Mikhael wrapped his hands around Alina's shoulders and leaned down. "We all need you to try, my Alina. If you want to go home in these clothes, with your hair in a bun and your face scrubbed clean, that's fine. But try."

Her lips mashed together in quiet refusal.

His grip on her shoulders tightened.

"It feels like just yesterday I watched you walk into the bakery in Kapotnya and I couldn't breathe because of the smile on your face. Today, I can't breathe because I don't know if I'll ever see you smile like that again."

Several feet away and eavesdropping like crazy, Vivian sniffled.

Alina brushed angrily at his hands, her own eyes dry but clouded over with quiet suffering. "Go and spend time with Bogdan while he is enjoying himself."

When he didn't move, she nodded in Vivian's direction. "We will keep ourselves—occupied."

Sensing he could push no further, Mikhael bowed and left.

ALINA

"SINCE SO MANY OF OUR FAMILIES COME WITH STRONG religious convictions," Vivian coaxed once she and Alina were alone, "the business attire is very modest. And most of it is donated."

Alina shook her head. "I don't want to take something that someone else could use. It sounds like these families come here with nothing."

"We only have one family in residence right now. A father and son. The mother didn't survive."

Fresh pain exploded in Alina's chest. She wondered if the boy who had lost his mother had loved the woman or if he was glad to be rid of her.

"You don't have to take anything with you if you don't want," Vivian continued as she took a few steps away from Alina. "But it doesn't hurt to try it on, see what styles you like before you do some shopping for yourself."

The pain as she imagined the boy and his dead mother turned to a defeat cemented in her chest. This woman was going to keep at her until she acquiesced.

"Fine," she mumbled and let Vivian lead her through a set of double doors and down a network of hallways until they reached a door marked "Wardrobe" in English followed by other languages in other alphabets.

Inside the room were racks of clothes. Vivian stopped at one filled with long sleeve blouses arranged by color. She pulled out a dark emerald top then disappeared into the next row. She re-emerged with a flouncy black skirt long enough to brush at Alina's ankles.

Seeing the expression on Alina's face, the woman offered a coquettish smile. "We'll just carry them with us for inspiration."

Alina's fingers danced against the plain black purse she had brought with her. Her new identity was inside, along with the smartphone Mikhael had secured for her. She didn't want to call him, just check the time and see how long this peculiar kind of torture had lasted so far.

Nearing the end of the wardrobe room, an elderly woman sat with a stack of papers. Vivian stopped and placed a hand against the older woman's shoulder, whispering in her ear. Glancing over, the other woman looked at Alina's feet and nodded.

Alina stalled. She couldn't do it, couldn't follow after this glamorous and clearly rich socialite with her foundation—and story of a dead husband—who wanted to dress Alina up for a day. Maybe the world worked like that when you grew up with money, when your own family hadn't scarred most of your body. But it didn't work in Alina's world. She would always know what was under the clothes.

It was time to make her apologies and go back to the main room or out to the car. Mikhael and Bogdan would find her when they were done, and she could apologize all over again.

"Please!" Vivian begged sweetly before Alina could open her mouth. "I don't want to overwhelm you. Let's go to the makeup chair and sit you down so you can relax."

The Lodge woman was little more than a stunted girl if she thought sitting down and playing with makeup solved real problems.

Alina shook her head and started to turn, her thoughts shifting to how to get back to the main room and then out to the car. Anxiety had dogged her each step of the way into and through the building and there was an even chance she'd take a wrong turn or two in her attempt to escape.

"I wanted to talk to you about Bogdan," Vivian said, expertly dangling the boy as bait.

"What about him?" Alina asked, turning back.

"Oh, something Reed and I were talking about." Giving no real answer, Vivian turned toward the makeup area.

Hooked, Alina followed after Vivian and let the woman place her in the seat.

"What were you talking about, what did Reed say about my son?" she asked after Vivian did a light facial cleansing without saying anything substantive.

"I heard that, on the trip back, Bogdan didn't want anything to do with anyone but Reed."

Alina nodded. The boy had spent a few seconds clinging to her when they were reunited, but when he realized she was working with the men who killed his "papa," he had instantly turned on her.

"Can I tell you something in confidence?" Vivian asked, her voice and gaze dropping.

"Yes," Alina answered flatly.

Whom did Vivian think she would tell anyway? Not Mikhael nor the boy, both of whom were as far out of her reach as they had ever been. Not the FBI, which only wanted to hear about the Rodchenko family. Certainly not anyone back east—she'd never made real friends because of Dima always spying on her and controlling her every move. And she wasn't supposed to contact anyone from her old life.

All secrets were safe with a woman to whom no one cared to listen.

Vivian exhaled a shaky breath, her hand pausing from applying brow powder. "Reed lost a child."

Alina felt like the room had started spinning around her. She didn't want to bond with this Lodge woman over death—first the husband, then the unnamed boy who had lost his mother, now Reed's loss of a child.

She didn't want to bond with Vivian at all.

Alina slid one leg to the side, ready to push up from the chair. Vivian's hand landed on her arm.

"Reed said you were willing to die to keep Bogdan safe and to get one last day with your son. He has the utmost respect for you because of that and knows you'll be a great mom for Bogdan. With his own loss, he's very observant on these matters."

Alina recoiled as the conversation turned even more uncomfortable. She was glad the boy was with Mikhael, not Dima. In the end it would work out between them. But there was no place in their lives for her. This beautiful woman on the verge of tears standing in front of her was just one example why.

She had seen the way Mikhael had looked at Vivian. The woman was whole. Alina was not.

"No, please," Vivian said, her fingers lightly pressing against Alina's shoulders so Alina wouldn't leave the chair. "I'll shut up."

She gestured at the mirror for more support. "I don't know any woman who wants to go out partly done."

No, Alina thought, her determination to leave crumbling as she caught her reflection. Half done was worse than never begun when it came to makeup. She had entered the room with dark shadows under her eyes and flaking, sallow skin from all the stress. If she left incomplete or without washing it off, she would look like a powdered corpse.

Surrendering once more, she waved a dismissive hand at the woman.

Another dozen or so minutes passed before Vivian pulled back, a closed tube of mascara in one hand.

"I'm guessing false eyelashes are a big no."

"Correct," Alina answered, her voice creaky from the silence they had fallen into.

"Okay, just this last bit then. Waterproof okay?"

Alina shrugged. She would prefer something she could wash off immediately if necessary, but her nerves were beyond frayed and the tears she had been holding back daily since the boy's last meltdown might come at any moment.

Leaning over Alina once more, Vivian used a lash curler, added a thin coat of mascara, used the lash curler again on the same eye and then laid down a thicker coat with a final curl before repeating the process on the other eye.

Finished, she rotated the chair so that Alina could look in the mirror.

Gaze unfocused, Alina slowly allowed the image of her reflection to sharpen and come together as Vivian brushed at her hair.

Alina looked from the expertly made up face down to the frumpy second-hand blouse she wore. She had allowed Mikhael to get the boy the kind of clothes to which he was accustomed, but she had insisted on going to the re-sell shops for her own clothing. Part of it was necessity. Finding long sleeves in late summer was hard.

The other part, the bigger part, was not unlike what had driven the boy to rub shoe polish in his hair. Before, she had only worn what Dima allowed—what he paid for. That meant drab cast-offs. For a while, he had insisted on sleeveless blouses exposing her scars except for when she visited the boy.

She took it all in even though she didn't want to, old pain soon mixing with new.

"Maybe just try on the clothes before I blow some curls in," Vivian said as she put the brush down and plugged in a blow dryer.

Alina's skin began to itch, her fingers absently scratching at her arms.

With no objection voiced, Vivian slipped out of the room for a second and returned with a box and plastic bag. She placed them on the counter then backed toward the door.

"I asked Carla to grab those before we came in here. No one will enter until you open the door. If you want to try it on and take it back off, that's fine—or if you don't want to try it on at all. Just give the idea a chance before you decide."

Alina remained frozen as Vivian left again. She stayed frozen for a few more minutes, only her eyes moving. The emerald shirt and long black skirt hung on the wall behind her. The box, its lettering visible through the thin plastic bag, contained shoes. A shiny black material she guessed was a bra or panties was also inside the bag.

She looked at her reflection again. The eyes staring back remained bone dry. With all the emotion running through her, she should have been crying. But even her emotions were arid—like she had felt them once but now they were only blowing back at her on a desert wind.

Sliding out of the chair on shaky legs, she locked the door and made sure there wasn't a second entrance. Returning to the makeup station, she pulled the box out first.

Fuck, the shoe box…

She had buried that memory so long ago—or tried to. Whenever she found herself recalling how she had fed the little mementos into the fire or the terrible thing that had happened after with the rabbit or Mikhael at the library, she pushed her thoughts toward the beating that had followed her father's discovery of her pregnancy.

It hurt less remembering how the electrical cord had lashed her body. That had been only flesh—not like losing the man she loved and cruelly hurting him to make sure he left, or how they had bragged afterward about setting the building on fire while he slept and of the big Russian's body pulled out of the rubble charred so thoroughly only his great size identified him.

Slowly, she peeled back the lid to find a pair of black suede shoes with a one-inch heel. Reaching into the bag a second time, she removed the black silky material, unfolding it to reveal a bra and panties, Vivian's expert eye having perfectly sized up Alina's measurements.

Slowly, she pulled the bottom hem of her blouse up over her head. Leaving her bra on, she shucked her shoes and pants off and stared at her scarred body in the mirror. The bra she wore wasn't from the re-sell shop, but it was a cheap eighteen-hour type in plain white cotton—a war horse compared to what Vivian had brought her.

Turning, she fingered the emerald green shirt. Smooth, lightweight and flowing like water, she wasn't certain what kind of fabric it was. She searched for a tag and discovered it was silk. Lifting a brow, she calculated that the shirt alone was more expensive than the entire wardrobe that she had rebuilt second hand, as small as it might be.

Silk shirts and powdered women were Mikhael's world—and Dima's.

Going back to the counter, she opened her plain black purse and pulled out the phone. Turning it on, she saw that an hour had passed. Shoving the phone back in the purse, she wondered what Mikhael was doing at that moment. Probably congratulating himself on his plan in bringing her here.

For some misguided reason, the fool thought he had a swan who was convinced she was a duck.

Reaching behind her, she unhooked her bra, her gaze avoiding the mirror as she put on the fancier undergarments and then the rest of the outfit. She would show him that if it walked like a duck, swam like a duck and quacked like a duck, it was a duck. No matter how anyone dressed it up or slapped makeup on it.

She would bear this last humiliation of trying to be what she wasn't and then he would see it was time to let her go and raise the boy on his own.

23

MIKHAEL

Sitting at the large conference table in Vivian's studio with his smartphone in hand, Mikhael thumbed through intelligence reports from work. Each day, the remains of what had been the Rodchenko empire crumbled a little more. The Grekovs were muscling in with some really nasty non-Russian motorcycle gangs in the U.S. There were at least half a dozen house fires from New York to D.C. in the last week that might not look connected to local investigators but were all properties that Dima had owned and used for everything from prostitution to drug warehouses.

Mikhael's bosses weren't pushing for him to return to work, but there was a lot of information to process and too few experts to do the job.

Hearing the studio door open, he looked up. Even

with Vivian standing at her side, he almost didn't recognize Alina. When he did, his heart seized.

Was there ever a more beautiful woman?

Pocketing his phone, he stood. Alina flinched. He didn't think she was afraid of him, just feared his inspection and judgment. So he approached slowly, his hands locked behind his back to keep from immediately touching Alina once he reached her.

"I'm going to see how Bogdan and Reed are doing," Vivian said, already slipping across the room to leave the two of them alone.

Alina stood with her gaze cast at the ground. He slid a finger under her chin but didn't force her to look up.

"What are you afraid of, my Alina?"

Maybe he had it all wrong. Maybe what she didn't want to see was love and hope shining in his eyes.

Gently, he pinched her chin between his finger and thumb, the pinch repeating again and again in a rhythmic caress. Her shoulders relaxed but she tried to tilt her head, to interfere with what he was doing.

"You look beautiful," he rasped softly. "Always, but I don't think you can see that."

"Stop trying to make me feel better, Mikhael," she said. "It's cruel, even if you don't mean it to be."

"How?" He pushed closer, his body brushing lightly against hers with each breath he took. "All I want is for you and the boy to be happy and safe."

"Take him and he will be," she persisted, pulling back, her hand instinctively searching for the handle of the door behind her.

He wanted to explode in denial but Bogdan rushed in at the other side of the room with Vivian and Reed in tow. He carried someone's smartphone in one hand and a mini hover drone in the other.

"Look!" he shouted. "Look what Reed gave me!"

The boy ran over, proudly thrusting the craft higher so his parents could inspect it.

"I have to transfer control to another phone," he explained then looked directly up at Alina. "Can I use yours, mama?"

"Of course."

Her voice sounded distant and Mikhael noticed that she still winced when Bogdan called her "mama." In the days since the boy had made his breakthrough, Alina hadn't sought to embrace him, either. At least she didn't withhold herself entirely. She would allow him to sit on her lap or rest against her when he wanted.

There was no doubt the boy wanted to be close to his mama. Alina's lap had become his favorite place to rest, his head on her shoulder and one hand curled around her arm. She would let him stay as long as he liked, often with him falling asleep on her and Mikhael carrying the boy to bed. But he feared Bogdan might relapse if Alina didn't begin to heal.

Still holding onto the drone and phone, Bogdan

kept staring up at Alina. A bigger smile brightened his already happy face and he put his arms around Alina's waist.

"You look so beautiful, mama!"

She stiffened, her hands stopping the instant before they would have closed around the boy's arms. Her gaze, loaded with accusation, shot first to Mikhael and then to Vivian and Reed.

Gently, she disentangled from Bogdan's embrace and shooed him toward Reed. Dipping into her purse, she handed the boy her phone. "You should switch it over now, in case it's difficult to understand."

As Bogdan walked over to the table with Reed and Vivian, Alina started to shake.

"No one put him up to that," Mikhael assured her. "He said it because he sees what I see."

She didn't answer, couldn't stop shaking. Grabbing her by the elbow, Mikhael walked Alina over to another door, one that led into a smaller, private space.

"We are borrowing your office, Vivian," he explained, his words clipped at the end.

Shutting the door, he tapped at a control pad on the wall, dimming the lights. A few more taps and soft instrumental music began to play.

"What are you doing?" The question emerged fast, almost breathless with an undercurrent of panic.

"Calming you," he growled, dragging her toward the sofa pushed against one wall.

"No—you are not," she laughed hysterically.

Plopping down, he pulled her onto his lap and wrapped his arms tightly around her chest as he had done that first month with Bogdan.

"I am not the boy," she protested, fear continuing to lace through her responses. "You cannot wrap your arms and legs around me and wait until I fall asleep."

"Bogdan," Mikhael rumbled. "His name is Bogdan and you haven't used it once in the last week. It means 'God rendered.' The one thing your papa let you do was name your son and that is what you chose."

She began to twist, but she was easier to keep hold of than their son. The boy's wild fury had powered his muscles as he thrashed and turned.

"No one told him to say that," Mikhael repeated. "He looked up and he saw his beautiful mama. Just like I saw my beautiful Alina."

She shook her head, the gesture angry. "It all washes off, you know. Clothes fade and wrinkle..."

Mikhael rotated her in his arms, defeating her attempt to escape.

"You are most beautiful bare," he said. "Raw...naked."

She dipped her head, refusing to look at him.

Hearing a sniffle, he relaxed his grip and tried to tilt her stubborn chin upward.

"Do not hide your tears from me, Alina. You have

to have someone you can cry in front of. Let it be me again."

"Your friend's efforts will be ruined," she rasped and pressed her cheek against his jacket.

Mikhael stroked at her hair, let her cling silently to him. He hummed softly to the music, his deep breaths keeping time. Warmth spread through him as she relaxed in his arms.

His Alina was letting him hold her and, for the moment, that was enough.

24

MIKHAEL

"Your friend is...sneaky," Alina said as Mikhael and Bogdan finished loading a box of clothes into the trunk of the sedan.

Mikhael smiled sheepishly. "Vivian's been called worse."

"Do you like the presents I picked out for you, mama?"

The boy was hugging her again, his arms around her waist. This time, she didn't look like she wanted to extract herself.

"Yes," she answered softly, her hand stroking at his head, almost a week's worth of growth giving it a velvety nap. "You have excellent taste for how to dress a lady."

Tilting his head up, Bogdan beamed a smile at her.

"In the car with you," Mikhael said, his gaze on the

clouds that had gathered while they were inside the facility. It looked like a strong storm rolling in from the east.

Gently manhandling the boy's head, he opened the rear door and steered him toward the back seat. "We'll get some food in your belly near Ashland."

Grabbing the car's frame so he couldn't be shuffled inside, Bogdan looked at Alina. "Can you ride in the back with me? I can show you the drone app on your phone."

Her jaw clenching with indecision, Alina finally nodded. "That would be nice."

Mikhael watched them climb into the back seat, Alina making sure the boy put his safety belt on before she let him start playing with the phone. Sliding behind the steering wheel, he caught her gaze on him in the rearview mirror.

She attempted a smile, the gesture hesitant and vulnerable, then returned her attention to Bogdan as he launched the app.

An hour later, they sat around a table at a Cracker Barrel, the boy wolfing down dumplings and chicken. Alina had ordered a pot pie, and Mikhael smiled to see her eating and not just pretending to eat.

Things weren't fixed. He knew that. But they appeared to be improving. The boy had built up a tough shell living under Dima Rodchenko's thumb, but, just like any other child his age, he wanted to be loved.

Mikhael didn't think Dima had ever offered Bogdan that emotion.

Alina would not heal as quickly, but he could see the fragile spark of hope in her gaze.

"Mishka," she softly chided as she gestured at his untouched food.

"Right," he grinned then shoveled some mashed potatoes and gravy into his maw. "Need to get moving soon."

"Yes." She cast a nervous glance over her shoulder. "The storm is still rolling in."

They finished their meal, returned to the sedan and beat the rain home, but not the wind. It battered at the windows as Alina made sure Bogdan brushed his teeth and changed for bed, then curled up next to him and read a few chapters from *A Bear Named Paddington*.

By the time she noticed Bogdan had fallen asleep, rain pattered softly against the windows—the larger storm still brewing beyond the city limits.

Leaving the boy's room, she paused next to the couch, her hands folded in front of her and her fingers lightly pinching at the cuff of their opposing sleeve.

"I thought I would try to fall asleep before the worst of it hits."

He nodded. They both knew she would be wide awake as long as the storm was nearby. Mikhael figured she wanted to avoid him, especially now that their son was in his room for the night. He wished she didn't need her space, but he would give it to her.

"Let me know if there's anything I can do," he said, watching her disappear into the bathroom.

Listening to water run in the sink, he pulled his phone out and opened a real estate app. So much was in flux, but he knew he needed to sell his one bedroom condo in Alexandria no matter what Alina decided.

He hoped she wanted to stay with him and for the two of them to raise Bogdan as a couple, not separately and definitely not her striking out alone in the world. But her staying was still a big "if" and he knew it.

Hearing her turn the knob, he put the phone down, his attention jumping to the bathroom door. She emerged, her face scrubbed clean of the cosmetics Vivian had applied. Alina's gaze bounced off him as she mumbled a goodnight.

He wanted her to look at him, to see in his face that he found her every bit as lovely as before she had washed the makeup away.

She simply wasn't ready.

When she shut her bedroom door, he sighed and turned off the couch-side lamp. Then he stood and went around the house, making the same checks he had when they returned from Dallas. Windows locked, security system armed, doors locked, land line working, the street clear of unfamiliar cars.

Going into his bedroom, he shut the door and

stripped down to his boxers. After turning off the light, he re-opened the door. In the dark, he settled under the blankets. Hands folded across his chest, he listened to the storm building in intensity and prayed his Alina would come to him as she had so many years before.

25

ALINA

Alone in her room, Alina listened to the storm intensify. Reaching blindly along the nightstand, she found her phone and pulled it under the covers. Clicking the weather app, she checked for flood and high wind warnings and wished the safe house had come with a basement.

Wouldn't that be the story of her life—to die from a tree falling on her room after Bogdan seemed to have finally accepted her as his mother?

Better pull back on that Russian fatalism, she scolded, clicking off the phone and returning it to the nightstand.

Thunder boomed, the sound waves rattling the window. She pressed her hands against her ears. The tactic only muffled the next clap of thunder. Sitting upright, she braced her back against the headboard and drew her legs up close to her chest. Her arms curled around her head as she pressed her face against her knees and began to pant.

You will not go to him.

She wanted to. Mikhael was the only one who had ever made her feel safe from the storms. He was the only one who had ever made her feel safe, period.

The window shook with more thunder. She trembled in response. When the noise subsided, she found herself stroking absently at the silk nightgown from the box of carefully folded clothes that Bogdan had helped select. The gown itself was sleeveless, but Vivian had been sure to include a matching long sleeve robe in a blush pink.

The smooth material soothed her fraying nerves until the next cracking boom. A half birthed shriek escaped. Diving under the blanket, she pulled a pillow over her head.

Had the thunder or her scream disturbed Mikhael? Was he awake and wondering if she would come to him?

Did he want her to?

Still sheltering beneath the pillow, she shook her head. He had said those things earlier to build up her confidence, to make her a better mother. For him to say she was most beautiful naked was ridiculous and had exposed his lies. That's why she couldn't go to him— she wanted it so badly it would kill her to be rejected or know that he was only playing along for Bogdan's sake.

That was what he was doing, right?

She slipped a hand under the nightgown, her fingertips skating lightly atop the surface of her scarred skin, feeling what Mikhael would feel if he reached beneath the fabric. She wondered when she had become such a coward.

With her chest muscles squeezing mercilessly at her lungs, Alina rolled out from under the bedding and sat up gasping for air. Pushing her feet into silk slippers, she pulled on the robe folded at the end of the bed.

Her feet tapped lightly against the rug, the music Mikhael had played in Vivian's office waltzing through her mind. It had felt so right for him to hold her, just as it had felt that night in the closet during the last storm, the two of them packed in like sardines.

As good as it had felt, she had still tried to push him away.

A roll of thunder shook the window, but she didn't jump, just stiffened as she kept the image of Mikhael holding her in the closet alive in her mind. If only she could survive on imagination and willful ignorance. She could pretend that Mikhael wanted her, that this wasn't just about "doing right" by her and the boy.

How many more years might they waste that way? Would it last until Bogdan finished high school or would they hold on tooth and nail until he graduated college?

God kept playing his drums, pounding away at the roof as the storm seemed to settle directly over the safe house for the sole purpose of magnifying her torment. She stood on shaking legs and walked toward the bedroom door. She would sit on the couch. The drapes were less lightproof in that room. She'd be able to count the seconds between lightning and thunder and brace herself.

Heading for the couch, she passed Mikhael's open door.

Did he leave it open for her?

No, she thought, he did it for the boy. Bogdan no longer needed locked down for the night.

Pivoting silently on one foot, she looked at the sleeping giant, his form faintly visible because he hadn't fully closed his curtains. He was on his back, the blanket folded all the way down toward the footboard, only the sheet around his hips.

His chest was massive, even bigger than when he was in his early twenties. She wondered what he had done to get so big. She wondered about many things. He had made powerful friends on the right side of the law—glamorous friends, too. He was supposed to be a charred corpse, but he wasn't.

How had he survived and then thrived? Did thriving include lovers? Was Alina's presence temporarily keeping him from the woman with whom he truly wanted to be?

She couldn't ask him any of those things. Some of the answers might crush her. Nor could she expect to get answers without having to respond to his questions, which would leave her mired in memories of pain and humiliation.

Retreating, she bumped a side table nestled against the wall. Mikhael slid immediately into a semi-upright position, his elbows propping him up.

"Alina?"

The question confused her. Her form was visible enough that even if his eyes were slow to adjust, it was clear she wasn't an intruder or their son. Had he been dreaming of some other woman—confusing the dream for reality?

"Yes, Mishka," she answered, her voice soft and uncertain. "I didn't mean to wake you. I was going to close your door so I wouldn't."

That was a lie. It slid out as easily as all the other lies she'd told him.

Lightning brightened the room through his open curtains. He patted the other side of the bed. "Come, wait with me until the storm passes."

Alina shook her head, her body clinging to the doorframe for support as she anticipated the thunder. "I have to get over this nonsense."

She had to get over all of the nonsense—the unreasonable fear of storms heightened by her half-brother's cruel practices and the idea that she and Mikhael could be bonded by more than raising their son as a unit.

"Do you have to get over it alone?" he asked and waited.

The sky roared before she could answer.

"I want you in my bed, Alina."

"Don't say it that way," she rasped.

Didn't he realize how easy it was for her mind to twist his meaning when his voice dropped low and caught on each syllable before releasing it?

"What way?"

A definite tease entered his tone. He patted the side of the bed as light flashed inside the room.

Damn, he was sexy. He had looked like a demi-god as a young man, with flawless skin, gracefully sculpted muscles and those piercing blue eyes. Now he was decidedly mortal, his muscles cut and shaped from steel, his jaw rough and his face lightly lined with a decade of time and scars. The combined effect made him brutally handsome and devastating to look at.

Her slippered feet crossed the room to stand by the empty half of his bed.

"It's going to crack and boom in five...four...three...two—"

Before he could finish his countdown, she jumped onto the bed and buried her face against his shoulder. Her arm curled around his neck as he hugged her tightly to him. When the sky roared again, she didn't nestle closer and shake.

Instead, she lifted her head and looked at him in the dimly lit room.

"Why aren't you married?"

His embrace tightened. His face pushed against the black veil of her hair.

"I do not think a lover should feel like they are someone's second choice" he answered, his breath filtering hot through the silken strands to warm her neck. "And that is all anyone but you can be—second choice."

"I wish that we could have…" Shaking her head, she tried to pull away from him but he wouldn't let her.

"Don't waste your wishes on the past, my Alina. Wish about the future then work to make them come true."

26

MIKHAEL

Rolling Alina onto her back, Mikhael pushed the hair away from her face and cupped her jaw. Lightning flashed. She tensed, but he wasn't sure if it was in anticipation of the next crack of thunder or because she didn't welcome his touch.

He started to hum, imperfectly recalling the music from that afternoon. The rough purr of his voice seemed to soothe her. The windows shook and she didn't seem to notice as much.

His hand slid from her cheek to the front of her neck, his thumb and index finger lightly tracing the contours then lifting to return a spot just below her chin and repeating the pattern. His back tingled with the knowledge that his bedroom door was open, but he didn't want to make her nervous by closing it.

In time, he would. Maybe not that night, but some future night. "One day at a time" he had once said to her. He had been both wrong and right. That was how they had survived her family, but it was no way to live.

Still caressing her neck, he kissed just below her ear. Her breathing melted, her breasts slowly lowering until all at once her lungs bottomed out and she seemed completely relaxed.

His cock responded to what felt like her surrender.

Oh, the things he wanted to do with her and the long hours he wanted to take doing them. He had experimented with a girl or two to stave off his hunger for Alina before that night in New York, but he had been green then compared to the experienced lover he had become.

He wanted to please her, to drape a carpet of ecstasy over her body that smothered her senses, driving her to the brink of annihilation before his soft kisses resuscitated her.

Sliding his hand along her collarbone, he dipped under the robe and curled his fingers around her shoulder.

Tensing, she tried to shrink away.

He withdrew, his hand on the outside of the fabric once more as he resumed the gentle humming.

"I want to touch you, love," he said when she had calmed again. "I want to stroke and kiss your breasts, your thighs. I want to taste you as I did before."

SCARRED

"Please," he said, his fingers glossing over her collarbone again.

Feeling her hesitate, he stopped.

"Do you know," she whispered after a few painfully long seconds, "that the French military helped invent Braille?"

Confused, he still managed a smile. His Alina had always been quoting him little facts from all her reading. Their new house would need a large library.

"No, I didn't," he murmured.

"Napoleon wanted something that could be read at night, without a light. A kind of code. So one of his men came up with what was called night writing. It was too complicated because you couldn't feel a symbol all at once."

"I see," he said and pressed his cheek against the curve of her neck.

"Do you?"

"I think so."

She was trying to explain why she didn't want him touching her, at least not directly on her skin. He had a feeling if he stroked at her with the fabric separating them, she would surrender again.

Slowly easing his hand within the folds of her robe, he found her shoulder and traced one of the scars detectible beneath his fingertips.

"This is your night writing," he said. "Even though I can't see the scars with the lights out, you're afraid what I might read while touching you, afraid of what someone else wrote on your flesh."

She let a shaky breath out that he took as confirmation.

Lifting his body up so that he leaned over her, his weight balanced on one elbow, he cupped her cheek with his free hand.

"You are the most beautiful woman I have ever known. The story your skin tells is one of love for our son and...I hope...for me. You were shielding our child, paying for your love for him when you weren't even allowed to acknowledge he was yours."

His thumb drifted up to stroke softly at the corner of her mouth.

"Do you really think some woman in a magazine or on television could ever match that?"

When she started to tremble beneath him, he didn't know if his words had made things better or worse. So he patted and smoothed at her hair and hummed again, some peripheral part of his brain aware that the storm had died out.

Alina pushed lightly at his chest, urging him away.

He surrendered without protest. He had damaged her in the past week from pushing too hard. He wouldn't keep repeating that mistake.

Quietly, she slipped out of bed and walked toward the living room. Reaching the doorway, she stopped.

Her hand curled around the knob, then she eased the door shut, the faint illumination from the window showing him she remained inside his room, not without.

Turning, she walked back to the bed and took off her robe. Shyly, she climbed onto the mattress and laid next to him on her side. Heart hammering in his chest, he turned to face her.

"Promise this is because you want me," she whispered. "Not because you think it will fix me or because you think we should raise Bogdan together."

"On my life," he promised. "It is because I want you, desire you. It has always been you, Alina."

Her eyes glittered in the dark. He thought he heard her sniffle as she maneuvered one arm between his neck and the bed and curled the other around his opposite shoulder.

"You were my only kiss," she said, the catch in her voice implying what he already knew.

He was more than her only kiss, he was her only lover.

"Then let me remind you what it's like to be worshipped by a man who loves you, my Alina."

She relaxed her grip on Mikhael. He guided her onto her back. Rubbing a soothing hand along her arm, he kissed softly at her cheek, starting near her ear and angling toward her mouth.

He bit once at the point of her chin before capturing her bottom lip. Her hands wrapped around his shoulders. He slid on top of her, his legs straddling hers and his weight resting lightly upon her. Trying to control his hunger, he buried his face against her neck. She pushed upward, her body instinctively knowing how to move against him.

Coiling his fingers through her thick hair, he gnawed at Alina's throat. Between them, his cock began to throb painfully as more and more blood flooded the already erect flesh. Growling, he straightened slightly and claimed her mouth with a hungry kiss.

His tongue swept in, darted back out as he bit at her lips, then plundered deep inside once more. She moved against him, her hips rolling and straining to stay in a constant grinding contact with his body.

Her fingers smoothed down the sides of his stomach then gripped his ass through the fabric of his boxers.

Shaking, he pulled back. "Baby, I'm going to explode if you touch me anywhere below my shoulders."

She laughed, almost giggled, and another shot of hard need penetrated his heart.

"Is it safe to touch you here?" Lifting her fingertips to his lips, she brushed a soft line from one corner of his mouth to the other. Closing his eyes, he tilted his head back and groaned.

"Not really."

"Okay." She clasped her hands together and drew them close to her chin. "Where should I put them, then."

A vision of her wrists bound and secured to the bed flashed through his mind.

"Here," he said, lifting her hands above her head, her pale arms framing her face as moonlight filtered through the curtains.

The position lifted her magnificently full breasts and made them strain against the nightgown's modest neckline. Shifting onto his side, he ran his lips across the silk fabric until he found the hardening point of one nipple.

Alina whimpered, her hips resuming their achy dance.

Teething lightly at her nipple and its breast, Mikhael smoothed his hand over the curve of her stomach to the top of her mound. With the gown still separating them, he began to rub. The gentle stroking coaxed her thighs apart. The strokes turned to kneading as he sucked at her nipple.

"Mishka," she softly keened.

He was going to pop just listening to her as she moved restlessly beneath his touch.

Pulling away for a second, he stripped out of his boxers and moved to the end of the bed. Grabbing her ankles, he spread her legs until they were fully open. His hands moved up her calves, pushing the gown as he went. His mouth trailed after, kissing at her knees, then her thighs until the fabric was bunched just below her hips.

"Lift for me, love," he entreated, every nerve ending in his body burning with the need for him to make direct contact with her pussy, to taste and finger and fuck her where she was wet and hot for his touch.

With a groan, she obeyed, her hands darting down to help him clear the fabric.

His mouth sealed instantly over her sex, his tongue taking charge of convincing his Alina just how much he desired and loved her. Her spine arched, forcing her bottom to dig at the mattress as her chest thrust upward.

She squeezed ruthlessly at her breasts, her hips locked in a pattern that had her mound bumping upward against Mikhael's face as suffocated groans wept past her pressed lips.

Thrusting two fingers inside her, he used them as an anchor to bring her back down to the mattress and hold her there as he began a more leisurely examination of her clit. He licked along its sides until she mewled. Next, he danced the tip just under the fleshy hood and its hidden pearl, making her growl.

"This then?" he teased before his lips captured the

hood and his tongue began to bully the small kernel all around its nest.

Alina stopped squeezing her breasts and seized Mikhael's head. He had thrown the clippers away after the shoe polish incident. There wasn't enough new growth yet for her to grab hold of his hair, so her nails scraped along his scalp.

He groaned against her flesh, the vibrations to the swollen, sensitive skin making her growl in return. His fingers began to move inside her. She was every bit as tight as he remembered, whereas he had grown larger in every measure.

Adding another finger, he curled his grip and gently twisted as he pushed in and out, his tongue busy licking a short, hard line over and over. He needed her wetter, needed the muscles too fatigued from orgasm to protest his entrance.

She moaned his name—the one only she called him by—as her hands moved to fist the fabric of the night-gown against her mound, her arms flexing to press down as hard as she could.

Inside her, he could feel the sharp contractions of pleasure as her climax began to build. Her legs trembled against his shoulders. Keeping her lips tightly sealed, she moaned and whimpered, her head beginning to thrash as if she wanted to howl.

He growled his own need to have her come, to be the one driving her onto the orgasm that rattled her bones and froze her breath before she melted into a raw, trembling mass.

"Mishka," she let slip again.

His free hand clamped down on her mound, his thumb extended to rub mercilessly at her clit as he lifted his head and looked at her writhe and groan.

"Stop fighting it, love," he begged. "Let me see you come."

His words seem to undo her. She cried out, her body locking in a paralysis of pure pleasure before her hips began to buck wildly and she screamed again, her hands clamped over her mouth to muffle the sound.

Waves of release rolled through her, her flesh under his command as he continued to stroke along her clit and twist three fingers thick inside her wet, clenching depths. Only when he was satisfied he could not wring another ecstatic sob from her lips did Mikhael gently return control of her body.

Her panting mellowed to slow, deep breaths as he settled beside her. With his lips pressed against her shoulder, his fingers traced her collarbone then drifted down to the peak of one breast.

Alina rolled to face him, a tease in her voice. "Can I touch you now?"

He cleared his throat, uncertain how to broach the topic of protection.

"Did I do something wrong?" she asked when he waited too long to respond.

"No, love," he hurriedly assured her, capturing one of her dainty hands and bringing it to his lips. "It's just that I don't know how I should proceed."

She giggled, the sound making his chest swell with joy.

"You don't mean you've forgotten? I haven't. Should I show you?"

Reaching between them, Alina captured his cock. He groaned, his entire body vibrating with the desire to bury himself inside her.

"I meant if you wanted me to use protection."

"Oh..."

Her grip on him softened and for a few seconds panic replaced the joy filling his chest.

"I think it's not about what we want right now," she continued, easing some of the tension her temporary retreat had caused. "But what effect it would have on Bogdan if I were to get pregnant so soon."

So soon?

Did that mean another baby—with him—was something she wanted?

Safely tucking that hope to the side, Mikhael cupped Alina's face. "So you would not be hurt or insulted if I happened to have bought some condoms recently?"

Even in the dimly lit room, he could see the scandalous shock spread across her face only to be replaced by a cheeky smile. "I would say your timing was presumptuous—"

"Pathologically optimistic," he countered.

She rejected his characterization with a short shake of her head, then snuggled up against him and planted a kiss on his neck, her mouth just below his ear.

"But I would also say I'm glad because I want you inside me. I want to make you feel like you just made me feel."

"Give me a second, then," he choked out before stumbling from the bed over to the dresser.

When he turned back to the bed, he caught her pulling the nightgown up and off, her voluptuous curves fully revealed by the moonlight darting past the clouds. Seeing him stare at her, she smiled shyly and drew her legs up.

He shook his head as he climbed onto the bed. His hands coaxed her knees apart and then her thighs. He knelt between her legs as he slid the condom onto his erection then flattened his body against the mattress to worship her with his mouth again.

With an aching slowness, he stroked and nibbled, nibbled and licked, his hands massaging her plump mound until she started to groan and shudder beneath his sensual ministrations.

Crawling up her body, he kissed her tenderly before gripping his cock and lining it up with her pussy. Feeling her hips lift, he cautioned her to go slow.

"Like this," he said, allowing just the head to rest against her opening.

Her chest bounced with an unexpected sob.

"So long I imagined us together, then I couldn't imagine anything. I thought I had gone frigid."

"Just dormant," he assured her. "Like a sleeping volcano. You are very much hot and ready tonight, my Alina."

Her head bobbed in agreement and he thought he saw the faint trace of tears as moonlight bounced off her face.

Wrapping her hands around his shoulders, she lifted briefly to draw him into a kiss. He let his weight press her back down to the mattress and pin her there as his tongue and cock began to tentatively probe.

Alina moaned into his mouth, her body still electric from the teasing preparations he had just put her through. She trailed her fingers down his shoulder blades, then his lower back before she cupped his muscular ass and squeezed.

Air shuddered from his lungs and through his constricted windpipe to release in an ache-filled wheeze as he fought for control. Slowly he pushed in, the crown breaching her tight opening. Then a little further, inch by swollen inch, letting her body adjust before he advanced. When he was balls deep, he let the weight of his lower torso sink him a little deeper.

"I'm stuffed," she said with a faint, rolling laugh that ended with another full throated moan.

Her muscles started to move around his shaft, gripping him like a fist and tugging with authority. She controlled him easily. He would have cut off a hand before willingly pulling out of her. Still, he retreated, just a little, and she rewarded him with a needy whimper and the threatening press of her nails against his bottom.

In he pushed, relishing her satisfied sigh as he stretched her again.

Damn, he felt like Superman—indestructible against everything but this woman moving beneath him, with him, her slick pussy twisting and pulling until his fat head rested against the mouth of her cervix.

His eyes rolled upward and a wave of dizziness washed over him.

Was his body actually threatening to pass out?

Yes. She did that to him.

"Mishka," she whispered, her lips against his ear as she strained upward. "Show me how hard you want me, how you can't hold back now that you have me."

Her words unleashed a beast inside him. He pulled back, the head popping free then pushing quickly back in, filling her with his full length, knocking at her cervix again as she knotted around him, her almost violent contractions milking him as he retreated once more.

A swift, hard return had her hands flying to wrap around the top of the headboard. Her hips lifted, slammed. A growl scratched its way up her throat as her breasts bounced and brushed against his chest.

Supporting his weight on one arm, he covered her hand with his, holding her in place as his hips took up a pounding rhythm that had them both moaning and grunting, their flesh rippling with need as the ache between them desperately scrabbled upward in search of its crescendo.

"Alina," he groaned one last time before his muscles locked and his shaft pumped out its release.

She quivered beneath him, eyes sealed shut and her voluptuous curves vibrating. Her hands slipped from his loose grip to run up and down his chest while she rode the last of her volatile climax calling out his name.

Claiming her mouth in a gentle kiss, he wrapped his arms around her as she collapsed against him.

Exhaustion sweeping through their bodies, he rolled onto his side and cradled her within the circle of his arms, his lips pressed against her temple. His mouth curved in a smile she could neither feel nor see as she slowly drifted to sleep.

There were more than just condoms hiding in the room, he mused. He had gotten a ring long before he had stopped to think about the need for contraceptives.

Reaching down, he pulled the sheet and coverlet up to their chins, Alina already asleep next to him.

Stroking her hair, he stared at her relaxed features and formulated a plan on how and when he would propose.

Leaning in, his lips ghosted hers with the night's final kiss before his whispered promise floated in the air above them.

"Soon, my Alina."

EPILOGUE

Alina

Their Home - Virginia

WITH SOMEONE'S FINGER STROKING LIGHTLY AT HER cheek, Alina jerked awake.

The textbook balanced on her belly started a slow slide toward the floor. Mikhael, the stroking culprit, scooped the book up and tucked a slip of paper between the pages to mark her spot. After placing the book on the coffee table, he held his hands out to help her stand.

"No more chapters tonight, love."

She indulged in a long, slow yawn before curling her hands around his. Finally on her feet, she clutched at his arms and tried to shake some feeling back into her legs. A glance at the clock showed that four hours had elapsed since she last stood. Almost an hour of that had been spent asleep.

"Bogdan?" she asked.

"Homework is done, teeth are being brushed."

Smiling, she tried to lean into him, but her belly blocked the way.

"Ooof," she complained, rubbing at the thing with its beachball shape.

"Just a few more weeks," he said, his deep voice rumbling with masculine pride at the baby growing inside her.

Mikhael brought her hands to his mouth just as Alina exhaled a nervous puff of air at the thought of giving birth. With his bright blue gaze studying her face, he planted soft kisses across her palms.

"It won't be like before, love."

Before had been a Russian midwife bribed to keep her mouth shut. *Before* had been no pre-natal care. *Before* was a memory and a topic that made her uncomfortable when Bogdan asked about his own birth.

At thirteen, he was fast becoming a man, but she still didn't think he was ready for that much truth. So her answer remained the same, her telling him that, like all things with the Rodchenkos, it had been hard and lonely, but worth it because it brought so much love into her heart.

"Don't be sad, mama," Bogdan said, coming into the living room and perfectly reading her expression. "It's all okay, yes?"

Her head bobbed, the smile she beamed at him

genuine. Drawing him into a side hug, Alina kissed his head, something that would not be possible much longer as fast as he was growing.

Seeing the book she had fallen asleep with, Bogdan picked it up.

"Will you teach me how to code? A first grader could do what Mr. Felts is showing us."

She nodded again, eyes misting with pride at how much he loved learning and how good he was at it.

"Oh no, *hormones*," Bogdan groaned when he saw her emotions getting the best of her.

Over the last few months, he had gotten quite good at recognizing the signs, even though he didn't know exactly what it was he was alerting Mikhael to when he'd order out with a stern, "Dad, you know what to do."

As he always did, Mikhael just chuckled under his breath before giving Bogdan a very G-rated reply, "First, I will tuck her into bed with a heating pad for her back. Then I will rub her feet until the 'hormones' are taken care of."

Bogdan accepted the proposed plan with an approving nod that had Mikhael chuckling again.

Tilting her head fondly at their adorable son, Alina rewarded him with another misty-eyed smile, even as her wayward thoughts began drifting over to all the ways Mikhael would often 'take care' of her pregnancy hormones in the privacy of their bedroom.

The heated way Mikhael was gazing at her wasn't helping her runaway thoughts one bit.

"Get your book bag ready and by the door," Mikhael said, lightly clapping Bogdan on the shoulder. "Then half an hour free time in your room before it's lights out and devices off."

The teen gave them another quick round of goodnight hugs then dashed to his room to deal with his bag. Alina waddled to the master bedroom and put on her nightgown as Mikhael made one final security check.

More than three years had passed and there had been no real threats to their safety. If she could believe Mikhael, there had not even been chatter picked up of anyone seeking to take revenge. Dima's top lieutenants had been as despised as he was—too despised to survive the power vacuum his death created.

Still, Mikhael checked the perimeter each night.

"What is that smile for?" he asked, coming into the bedroom and closing the door behind him.

"For you," she answered, sliding beneath the covers and patting his side of the bed. "Our mighty protector."

A soft grin lit his face but he didn't immediately join her on the bed. Stepping into the walk-in closet, he pulled off his shirt, then his jeans. Alina's body twisted the entire time so she could watch each item removed, each muscle revealed.

Turning to find all her attention on him, he chuckled, cupped himself and threw a subtle wink in her direction.

She plopped back on her pillow with a dreamy sigh followed by a giggle.

"This baby will need to be born on time, not a day later," she declared as he climbed into bed to join her. "It's been so long since I have felt you inside me. So very, very long…"

Mikhael cuddled her side, hand sliding down and over to reach between her legs and stroke at her flesh, fingers dipping to find her absolutely drenched for him, of course.

"Alina, my love, I'm starting to think you say these things to get me as worked up as you are," he accused with a doting smile, and a hardening erection nudging against her hip.

Guilty as charged. It worked each time, too.

She defended her actions with another declaration that, despite its double meaning, wasn't at all teasing. "You always know just how to make me happy, Mishka." Then with another bout of hormones hitting her, she couldn't help but ask, "Are you as happy as I am?"

Eyes tenderly locked on hers, he replied softly, "For ten years, that word didn't even exist in my vocabulary, or my life. Each day now, I think I can't possibly feel any happier than I did the day before. And each day, you and our son prove me wrong."

When a river of emotions began spilling from her

eyes in earnest, he kissed her tears away before sealing his lips over hers to ground her the way only he could.

"Now lay back, love. I believe it's my turn to make you endlessly happy right now."

— The End —

———

Continue the *Savage Trust* series
with

<u>FRAYED</u>
(Trent & Daniella)

Daniella Marquardt has one stop to make before she can flee the state with her newborn niece—a baby with a price tag on her life and no one to protect her. Along with money and hope, time is something Daniella doesn't have a lot of. Still, she needs to find the last man to see her sister alive. To thank him.

Trent Kane doesn't know what to make of the woman standing in his office preparing to go face certain death armed only with a plan that has no chance in hell of working. When he learns her connection to the infant he recently saved, the solution is simple; she's getting his help, whether she wants it or not.

As far as Daniella's concerned, trusting this bossy, hardened, brutally protective stranger is never going to happen. He may be the big, bad Chief Operating Officer of a private military firm with unlimited resources, but he's also the coldest—albeit, intensely compelling—man she's ever met.

The way Trent sees it, this woman effectively turning his life upside down is a risk to herself, and him as well. Despite everything, she still believes in love, which tells him she has no place in his world. Precisely why he needs to ignore their dangerous chemistry and quit being so damn attracted to her.

But, as hell begins to rain down all around them, one thing becomes evident very quickly.

They're both going to fail at their well-laid plans.

Available Now

ALSO BY CHRISTA/C.M. WICK

the FAR TOO TEMPTING *collection*

Tempted Beyond Reason (*Wake & Lacey*)

Tempted Beyond Relief (*Wylie & Rhea*)

Tempted Beyond Return (*Logan & Lily*)

———

the UNTOUCHABLE CURVES *collection*

Curvy Attraction (*Aiden & Cecelia*)

Curvy Seduction (*Owen & Gemma*)

Curvy Perfection (*Cayce & Ashley*)

and

His Curvy Temptation (*Declan & Melanie*)

[an *extra curvy* Untouchable Curves standalone novel]

———

the IRRESISTIBLE CURVES *collection*

Chasing Her Curves (*Hawk & Ginny*)

Claiming Her Curves (*Blake & Pippa*)

Capturing Her Curves (*Shane & Velda*)

and

Keeping Her Curves (*Ian & Juno*)

[an *extra alpha* Irresistible Curves standalone novel]

————

the HIS TO CLAIM *series*

Book 1: **Every Last Touch** (*Walker*)

Book 2: **Every Last Look** (*Barrett*)

Book 3: **Every Last Secret** (*Sutton*)

Book 4: **Every Last Reason** (*Emerson*)

Book 5: **Every Last Call** (*Siobhan*)

*BONUS FREEBIE (big brother Adler & Sage's standalone
novel: Every Last Doubt) available FREE at*
christawick.com/free

————

the UNTIL YOU *series*

Unraveled (Corwin & Belle)

Unveiled (Lucas & Theresa) *all new story!*

Untapped (Teague & Charlie)

————

a STANDALONE CROSSOVER *novella*

Hot Nights Winter Lights *all new story!*

[*with character cameos from 3 different series*]

———

CHECK OUT CHRISTA'S DARKER, *DIRTIER* SIDE

WRITING AS C.M. WICK

The Contract (Beckett, Jace, and Gabby)

[a standalone *ménage*]

Tempted By Trouble (*Austin & Gina*)

[a standalone erotica]

———

the SAVAGE TRUST *series*

Wrecked (Luke & Marie)

Scarred (Mikhael & Alina)

Frayed (Trent & Daniella)

———

the SAVAGE HOPE *duet*

His Trust (Collin & Mia, Book 1)

Her Heart (Collin & Mia, Book 2)

---

the DARK & DIRTY ALPHAS *series*

Her Only Choice (Maddox & Carson & Regina)

Join my EMAIL LIST to get new release & sale alerts!

THANK YOU FOR READING & REVIEWING!

Thank you so much for reading. I hope you enjoyed the story and will consider taking a quick minute to drop off a review at the eretailer where you purchased this book. Every single review means so much to me, and helps us authors so much in terms of book visibility. Reviews not only affect online presence on eretailer search engines, but also marketing/promotion opportunities as well. And most of all, it helps readers like yourselves find books and authors. It's one of the best ways you can support us indie authors and help our books find their way into more readers' hands. Review or not, I appreciate all of you readers for continuing to hang out with the characters in my head and letting me continue to do what I love.

ABOUT THE AUTHOR

New York Times and *USA Today* bestselling author Christa Wick has been hybrid publishing since 2012 (yep, she's one of the O.G. indie authors). She's written 50+ romances starring curvalicious heroines and alpha-licious heroes whose stories span the spectrum of: steamy & sweet, steamy & emotional, steamy & suspenseful, steamy & paranormal, steamy & dark, and…well, you get the idea. She also writes sci-fi thrillers and suspense novels under other pen names.

New Release & Sale Alerts
→ *bit.ly/ChristaWickEmailList*

Get my FREEBIES!
→ *www.christawick.com/free*

Where to find me & my books:
→ *www.christawick.com*
→ *facebook.com/christawickbooks*
→ *bookbub.com/authors/christa-wick*
→ *bit.ly/Books2Read_ChristaWickLinks*

→ *goodreads.com/christawick*